DELETING

VINCENT

A FEMALE KILLER'S CONFESSIONS

MYFANWY J. WEBB

First published 2025

Rockpossum Publishing

A catalogue record for this book is available from the National Library of Australia.

ISBN 9780645277555

Cover Design by Myfanwy J Webb

This book is dedicated to those people believed
to have taken their own lives, but in truth are victims
of homicide.

CHAPTER 1 POSTMAN

IN OCTOBER OF 2007, SPRING DISPLAYED HER wares in the form of bouquets of beautiful native flowers in the bush nearby. Red and white grevilleas and yellow wattles dotted the scratchy heath along the coast. The red waratahs on the road to the nearby river village of Patonga had nearly finished their striking bloom. My boyfriend and I had planted native bottlebrush plants near the council strip to give some privacy to our house from passers-by. These flowered profusely during the spring of 2007.

A few weeks into October, the postman rode his motorbike to a stop in front of the mailbox as I walked up the driveway towards him. Instead of forcing it roughly into the small box as usual and bending everything badly in the process, he uncharacteristically waited and handed the envelopes directly to me. I expect that he paused to allow himself more time to take in my short skirt and skimpy halter top that barely cradled my two rather large girls. This bloke who seemed fiftyish, I long ago had pegged as an arrogant, chauvinistic, leering pervert. He usually couldn't care that he daily, chewed up the lawn in front of the mailbox and made a sandy rut with his tires as he stopped his motorbike. All due to the unnecessary speed he rode at.

Something about him that spring day reminded me very much of my best friend Debbie's revolting psychiatrist boyfriend. It was Thursday and my boyfriend stays out at the pub on a Friday night. Before I knew it, I pushed my chest out as I neared the creep and, smiling, I touched the back of his hand as I took my mail from his outstretched arm. He allowed himself a long deep look down into my cleavage and then made some comment I cannot remember about the bottlebrush flowers flapping next to the mailbox. Before I knew it, I asked him if he wished to join me alone sometime to see some more gorgeous flowers, not far from here, up in the bush. He agreed. I said I'd let him know tomorrow where and when. Away he went.

Next day, as I heard the motor of his bike becoming louder, I sauntered out to meet him. As he handed me the mail, I seductively whispered to him,

"Seven tomorrow at the Umina skate ramp."

He grinned, nodded and rode on. I had spent much of the previous night working through the plan in my head. Dying from exhaust gas in a car is very intentional and unambiguous as suicide. That's why I chose it as the mode of suicide for the postman.

Somehow it came together for me rather fast paced. All I had to do now was work out the details of the things I'd need. In the privacy of the garage, I measured the diameter of the exhaust pipe on the car. Then I stretched the tape measure along the side the car to the front door. On a note pad, I scribbled the measurements down and added the word "gloves, "baby wipes, "belt" and "bourbon cans". I guessed he'd be a bourbon drinker, or an anything drinker. I ruminated on the exhaust bit for a while. What do I use as a joiner piece from the actual exhaust pipe to the garden hose I'd chosen to use? What's something that wouldn't melt straight away? What the hell do people use? Looking around the garage, I couldn't see any bits and pieces that would work. Probably because our garage was tiny and only fitted the car, we hadn't accumulated much junk around the place. I look at the car and think there are tubes and pipes all under the bonnet that must handle high heat from the hot engine. I popped the bonnet to have a look. There is a wide black shortish tube, say a ruler length long near the radiator with a big bend in it. A hose pipe. Pushing down on that I discover it is rubber and a bit flexible and seems wide enough to stretch over the exhaust pipe. The tape measure confirms it. So, one end over the exhaust pipe and I can stick garden hose through the other end and wrap the joined part with that thick silver-grey wide duct tape I've seen in the hardware. Wrap it around and around to seal the gasses in. I added hosepipe to the list. The more I can have it seem to actually work, the more authentic the whole thing will appear. It's not till much later that I realise a potentially serious blunder here. He won't be inhaling any exhaust, so carbon monoxide gas won't be in the body and an autopsy will show this.

6

While carrying out these actions, I felt a little smug somehow. No one knew my thoughts and plan. The secrecy gave me powerful superior feelings about myself. Only two people would know the plan, him and me. Flashes of Debbie's useless boyfriend's face momentarily sneered at me. These flashes became more frequent as I proceeded with my plan. At the shops, I carefully selected the goods and chose the widest softest belt I could find. Back at home, I rang Stuart, my boyfriend.

"Heh, sweetie, it's just me."

"What's up babe?"

"Can you get some milk on your way home?"

"Yeah"

"And are you going to the pub with Jacko and crew tomorrow night?" I asked, rather smoothly I thought.

"Yep, don't worry about dinner for me tomorrow, I'll be pretty late like last week."

"Righto, see you tonight then Stu."

"Yep bye."

So that's him out of the way. No factory shifts tomorrow either.

That night, I still remember how disbelief punctuated my thoughts. Disbelief at myself for thinking this thing through with detail let alone buying the gear! The only way to carry through, became an overbearing detachment from my other self. This more powerful me chastised the other pathetic one. I could hear the put downs ricocheting around within my skull. All the actions surrounding the plan began to fuel a powerful feeling. It will be the way to rid my head of Vincent's filthy ugly face forever.

CHAPTER 2 OLD LADY

HOW DO PEOPLE FEEL DEEP WITHIN THEIR CORE when they take absolute control of another person's life? Today is the day. I have prepared and I will be exhilarated. They were my thoughts on that otherwise typical, spring day in 2007. A day forever permeated by the smell of peppermint and wet eucalyptus. A day I wish never happened.

Ø

I often think how if only five years earlier, I had not driven to the neighbouring suburb early that morning to shop and had instead patronised my local shops as usual, then life may have been very different for myself and many other people. I would not have driven by that ugly red brick villa with the old man screaming on his knees on the dirty, sandy council strip.

"She's dead!" "She's dead!" The old man had said over and over.

I walked from my car across the grass towards him. He grabbed my arm and twisted me around, nearly losing his old man type cap from his head in the process, to guide me towards the house entrance. Saying,

"She's in there, my girl, she's killed herself." He practically pushed me towards the open front door.

I turned to look at him as he let go of me, and his fat, white, flabby face had a pained, desperate look that made me feel plain annoyed at him. His ugliness and lack of composure left me feeling scarce respect for him. One thing I knew is he presumed I entered the house to help him. It was curiosity and a shade of excitement at actually seeing someone dead that drew me in. I also thought the hopeless bloke would more likely stay outside and away from me if I looked inside, which he did.

Next to the kitchen slotted a small bedroom containing a double bed pushed up against a window. When I entered, I smelled old urine and new vomit. An elderly woman lay on her left side in an awkward pose on the unmade bed with her head flung back on the pillow. Frilly apricot-coloured curtains behind the bedhead framed her round face. Her pale blue eyes were open and staring unseeing at the wall. Black pupils filled half the eye. I could not see the bad skin, hollow cheeks of a junky. I could see however, on the worn carpet, empty prescription blister packets surrounding the bed and next to a small upturned bedside table. She had a sickly grey-green pallor and stiffened limbs. She lay there very dead. Involuntarily, my hand reached out to touch her bare arm. My fingers felt the cold flesh. I pressed down with my index finger to explore the hardness of the tissues. Intrigued at the greyness of her skin, I wondered how much blood would now be clotted in her right side after gravity pulled it down through her vessels. Looking at her soft round face and frizzy blond permed hair, she reminded me of my best friend Debbie, and I thought about how this elderly woman is the age Debbie deserved to live to be, rather than be removed from the earth at twenty-four. Never to grow old.

Experiencing a pang of protectiveness for this old lady, I also thought how the old man with his flat newsboy cap reminded me of a greyhound owner I used to know and hate. As a former veterinary nurse, I was the one forever euthanising his dogs.

Voices right behind me broke my reverie. In one smooth action, my hand moved up to her eyes and I forced her eyelids down just in view of a police officer who walked through the bedroom door and asked me who I was.

I answered calmly, explaining how I wished to help the poor hysterical gentleman outside. What astounded me at that moment was how quiet my voice sounded which contrasted completely with how I felt. My heart thudded against my rib cage and sweat began to trickle on my forehead. As the uniformed man talked at me and asked me questions, I answered unthinkingly while focusing my thoughts on the corpse.

"Suicide." A man's gruff voice interrupted us. The word said with an unmistakable dismissive tone.

"There's a note and some gifts set out for various people on the laundry bench here," he went on.

"Typical oh dee this one. Nothing sus here. We don't want to go worrying those busy boys upstairs with this one. We learnt what shit happens when we called in that last job."
A policeman's stern face peered into the room, looking closely at the medication packet on the carpet.

"Empty blister packs in the bedroom. Yeah, Pethidine."
This workmanlike atmosphere that the police officers produced, hung with monotony, intrigued me. I imagined these men could easily sit behind an office desk with an identical demeanour.

Unexpectedly, the haggard tear-stained man entered the room yelling how she would never leave him. The officer I had spoken to, shifted abruptly to a sympathetic mode. With an ever so slightly patronising tone and with a barely concealed tiredness, he explained, as if by rote, to him that he, in his many years of policing, could assure him that his wife most definitely did take her own life and blood tests would confirm this. Over the years, he had handled many identical cases. He should prepare himself for the need for a routine autopsy with this one falling into the category of sudden death. The distraught man softened and said,

"You'll find the doctor's drugs in her. She was addicted and ate them like lollies. Maybe her pain just got too much for her."

It was not clear whether he meant physical pain or mental anguish. Remembering my presence still in the house, the gruff cop told me I could leave now. When I failed to move, for the second time in less than an hour, a man clutched my elbow. He steered me out and down the steps. At the same time, I kept thinking what if it was really the wife that had got too much for the old man? That lady's kids, if she had any, would always believe that she abandoned them, and the truth would forever be concealed from them. I thought of Debbie and her fiancé Vincent. It cannot be that easy surely! Vincent concealed his killing of Debbie. With disinterested police like these ones, I observed today, I can see how easy it is for people to get away with taking someone's life.

6

Since I was a kid, I had often wondered how corpses look. More recently, whenever a car crash presented itself on the road ahead, I would slow down and peer into the mess of metal hoping to catch a glimpse of pale skin splattered with blood or a lone leg lying on the tar with a shoe on the end. Once, while at the nursing home wasting time with my demented, old grandfather, I heard excited voices down the corridor. Tracking the noise to a room, I stopped in the doorway. Looking in, I could see a body-sized bulge under the white sheet that stretched over the head. I leaned on the door jamb staring. A sour-faced nurse whooshed towards me and slammed the door so fast I leaped backwards and fell over. After that, at every visit thereafter until the old boy died, I would pretend to become lost and wander around looking for beds with sheets covering people's heads. I never found one. At school, I would interrogate my friends about their deady bones experiences, like when Andrew McKalif saw someone's actual brains spilling down a dark country road one night after a drunk driver had lost it round a bend.

Touching that first corpse sparked a hellish chain of horrendous events that unfolded five years later when I first

8

pictured myself doing harm to another, I was completely disgusted with myself. It is like I involuntarily had to listen to two of my own voices. One saying, get real Ashli you have got to be kidding. What are you thinking? You cannot be serious! Just forget that forever. Then the other one saying, well fuck it. Why not just imagine it? Thoughts do not hurt anyone, and no one will ever ever know my thoughts if I never open my mouth and speak them.

That is how it started. A context of harmless, seemingly innocent, imaginative fun that became feral, then somewhat obsessive, then all-consuming till my mind was absolutely encapsulated like a silkworm's thready mass of a cocoon holding it completely still. I dared to delve into the inner reaches of what I could be capable of, but with dire consequences. If I believed in God, then I would say that Satan's claws certainly penetrated through to my heart and froze it. That is how it felt. To become so frozen though, took significant effort from me. That might sound strange that there was effort. I worked and struggled to become so bad but that's part of the conflict between my two selves. The good self, let's call her Glinda like the good witch in the movie The Wizard of Oz, is the stable self, knowing right from wrong, but the bad self, I'll call her Evillene, also from the 70s movie, known as the Wicked Witch from the West, claims to not have knowledge of right and wrong. The two fight, with Evillene gradually over time suppressing Glinda. The struggle is to hate the people enough to do the deeds to them. To be able to do the hideous things, I had to tell myself, sort of brainwash myself that I completely despised these humans. My mind would produce reasons that built upon other reasons as to why these people were scum and did not deserve to be treated humanely. This process did not appear to me consciously but manifested into a compulsion not unlike my liking for drinking alcohol and becoming drunk. An alcoholic knows, if they are not in denial, then that one drink is too many and two are never enough. For me, one thought is too many but two are never enough. Once I started with the contaminated germ for the idea, I found a desire and unrelenting need to see it go as far as it could. At first, the thirst felt quenched just playing it out in detail in my mind, but later, the anticipation built up so much that I felt compelled to play it out in cold, hard reality. After a while, no off switch existed, no buttons in sight for me to switch the process off. Nothing. No control.

I say that I think there are a lot like me out there, because I am not that different to the average person. As a child I grew up in the suburbs, loved animals and like so many girls, dreamed of being a veterinary surgeon but of course my grades were way to low so ended up working as a vet nurse.

It is like, well if I can go that far, to those extremes then anyone with the right set of circumstances could do the same. I would say a person's behaviours can either expose or protect them from arrest. Behaving average is the best cover. To give you an idea of the contrasting selves becoming the ultimate protector from capture, the sweet-as-Glinda girl appeared to the wider world as relatively quiet and normal. She exhibits the same difficulties as the average person. People, I like to think, could relate positively to various aspects of my personality. Generous. I lavish friends and family with expensive presents at Christmas or Birthdays. Friendly. Small talk usually bores me, but I am the queen of small talk when I am in the mood. I can smile as sweet as a flower and compliment some old hag in the chemist on that 'gorgeous, coloured blouse' while all the time feeling completely superior and thinking to myself what an ugly, fucked up, wrinkled and dumb, old hag she is and how can she be bothered even speaking when she lives such a detestable life as hers. That can give me a hit, albeit cheap, laying it on thick sometimes. I have always enjoyed this. Once at a party, to bring this nerdy, dick shit down a notch, I had a little play with him. He revealed himself in an arrogant manner, to be studying mathematics, so I pretended to be that one in a million girl that truly understood his nerdy passion. I could see he was overwhelmed with admiration and surprise when I told him about my favourite number being some prime number. It was seven or eleven, anyway he said his favourite was a prime number too. I could tell, he was completely genuine about this. The banter went on a bit, till I became bored and then I could not rid myself of him, so I told him that I really hated maths and it's always been my worst subject blah, blah. He became rather angry with me but luckily, I'd been at the party long enough anyway, so I left him to his humiliation. Looking back on that incident now, I can see that the poor bloke became victim to an immature girl who could well have fucked him up for the next string of chat ups by chicks for the measly price of my cheap thrills. Now, I tend to restrain myself in letting on to the recipients of my superior feelings towards them.

Cops not bothering to investigate equivocal suicide/homicide cases properly and assuming suicide is known to happen. People just do not know how often it happens. Authorities assumed for years, for example, that the double murder by dentist Colin Howell in Ireland in 1991 of his wife and lover was a double suicide. He pleaded guilty to homicide in 2010. And in May 2022, an Australian man was finally convicted of murdering the American student Scott Johnson in 1988. It was an assumed suicide with the victim's clothing and belongings found at the top of a cliff. It took years of campaigning by Johnson's brother to have the case reinvestigated. Maybe Australian police are less diligent than other countries. Or perhaps their training and protocols are different, and the general duties officers just need more specific questionnaires to help direct them in separating suicides from murders.

According to the FBI in America only half of all homicides are solved but the National Homicide Monitoring Program in Australia suggests that the percentage of homicides that remain unsolved in Australia is around twelve percent. These though, are only the deaths deemed homicide. Too many assumptions are made by authorities about serial killers, and it is like leaving holes in a fishing net for the fish to escape through. The net will hold certain types of fish, the big and easy to catch species, but the net releases the smaller slippery ones. It is so bloody easy to do this stuff without people ever suspecting. Looking back at it all now, that is the scary thing. See how far backpacker serial killer Ivan Milat got before he was finally reeled in by the police.

6

My life before my descent could be described as straightforward enough. My home life entailed a devoted boyfriend, a fulltime job, albeit a bit crappy as a factory worker, enjoying the sport of surfing and a social life. I think that may have been part of the problem for me. Feeling as though I am not a mundane person and yet here, I was, living a mundane existence. When I analysed my life, the constraints on the way I wanted to live seemed to increase in number the more I thought about it. It felt like a sniper was gradually shooting out all my freedoms in life and there did not seem to be anywhere for me to move out of his glowing red sights. A kind of non-conformist from childhood, this suffocation did not sit well with my psyche.

At work my friend Melita understood me. Well, only to a point. We both worked at a local cake factory on eight-to-twelve-hour shifts, rostered four days or nights depending on the contracts the factory ran each week. With these long hours and being paired up together on the floor working the same conveyor belts, we had a lot of time to discuss many topics. She seemed to get me somehow even though our backgrounds differed dramatically. A small, stocky pretty girl of Maori descent, she could fire up like me, but she and I would heat up about the same things, unlike most of the other people working there. The bulk of workers were menopausal cranky, bitchy women. Not a lot of fun to work with, mainly as they had chips on their shoulders, and they were plain fucking dumb. I should say deaf and dumb because most had industrial deafness too. The machinery was so loud we had to wear earmuffs that never stopped the hearing loss. Their hierarchy bothered me. To me, we all worked in the same shit hole doing the same crap work and so that leveller should provide enough camaraderie amongst everyone. No, the suckers who had been there the longest held the stripes, or should I say the helmets. Years ago, the company gave white helmets to the workers so if you wore a helmet, then that indicated you had worked in the place a long time and longer than most. This meant you were top of the heap. To me, helmets just indicated the biggest suckers.

As far as explaining why I began descending the life trajectory that I did, I have to say I am not sure why, but a few variables merged during 2007. Three elements of my life swirling around started me thinking outside my usual way. The work at the fucktory as Melita and I liked to call it, started to make me aggressive, unsettled, and rebellious. I resented stepping down a few status rungs to work in a factory when my previous work was as a veterinary nurse. I resigned as a nurse because euthanizing the endless stream of well-behaved racing greyhounds became too much for me. At the fucktory, we were continually being reminded of all the bloody rules. Do not eat the food, don't walk down the path where the forklift goes, don't this, don't do fuckin that. My excitement entailed how many rules I could break in a shift without people knowing. My boyfriend thought I would be caught stealing all the pocket pies as we called them, and I would be sacked. Our white, greasy uniforms had pockets in the front simply perfect for slipping small pies in. The condescending airs of the women there made me increasingly angry and my default response of just copping their crap started to gnaw at me. Pressure in my head accumulated every time some old cow told me off and I said nought.

Then there was a string of traffic fines. Fine number one in January in Mann St, Gosford Central Business District for parking my car too long. Why the hell can I only park for thirty minutes and not thirty-five? What really is the issue with that? Then, a cop in an unmarked dark grey Holden booked me for driving slowly across a clear pedestrian crossing even though the person had already crossed and no one else was in sight. The traffic light displayed red not green, and that was the problem. This seemed ridiculous to me. Then in March, another policeman pulled me over and booked me for overtaking a very slow truck travelling to Woy Woy. Because I had momentarily driven beyond the speed limit while I did this, and it happened to be the piece of road over the narrow Rip Bridge, then he could make me pay a hefty fine. That bridge used to have a broken line indicating overtaking available, but that was changed. So speeding and dangerous driving, overtaking on a solid line. Rules, stupid rules. Pay or attend court. Who wants to waste precious time in court?

My life when I analysed it, bored me stiff. I could not feel anything. I did not feel like I was real. The fucktory work for me really, was a form of mental torture. My surfing was failing to progress, and Stuart my boyfriend kept stressing that I would lose my job if I didn't do what I was told. I was increasingly being told by Stu, supervisors at work, cops, men all over the place really, to toe the line, play the game, bloody do what you are told or else. Or else what? I suspect somehow all these things coalesced and thus became the catalyst for a major shift within the way I looked at the world and how I lived in it. I just thought, well rules are just constructs made up by society. We choose, or choose not to, live by them all. Why not ditch some big ones? This might make life exciting if I can break out of some of the brainwashed ways of thinking and acting.

As my mind scanned through the variables a certain confidence grew. Many people do things that are quite dramatic and are never caught. Why not I? Many dumb people even do serious stuff and evade capture. I am intelligent enough and so surely must have a better probability of success. The other thing is I don't have a criminal record. This, I believe, is a significant advantage for me. I have always thought cops are lazy. I reckon they assume an unrealistically high proportion of people who break the law are actually caught. There is no way to determine the true proportion of people that are busted for their criminal activity. Estimates suggest the cops only solve two per cent of major crimes. A cleanskin as they call them, are people whose offending actions are assumed to be most likely a one-off occurrence, as these individuals are not in the system and have never been in trouble before. This assumption is bolstered if other aspects of the individual are considered not shady at all. So, investment of energies by police, often perhaps target those who do have a record in the system because they think they have a higher chance of continuing crime behaviour than those never actually caught or convicted. Or their cognitive bias says to them that the probabilities are higher for the one with the record. The cohort of those repeat uncaught offenders maybe do not always have clear indicators of criminality, unlike the usual roughies. This is another reason some police perhaps don't waste time on cleanskins and move onto convicted criminals. Why delve into unlikely people for a crime when there are plenty of more likely people to invest your time at work on? It surely must be more difficult to gain information on people who are not on the database than people with a record, splattering data everywhere about their misdemeanours.

The form of my dissenting descent, if you like, began as imagination. It's not like I consciously decided that 'oh okay this is what I'm going to do now to spice up my life', it's more that when someone annoyed me, I was instantly reminded of a man I knew in the past. I then started to feel in control of my universe as I imagined plotting the course of someone else's demise but more specifically, this certain man. However, a sort of angst crept in too. The more I imagined stuff, the more my best friend Debbie's round face and her frizzy blonde hair would flash before me at the most inopportune times. This became disconcerting. The images and the man who I deemed to be her killer, also began to surface even to the extent that I would awake at night, smelling the scent of the man's cheap aftershave. When this happened, I would think how it is all ok. I am not doing anything bad by daydreaming, even if it had now permeated my subconscious. I am just thinking through what it would be like to end someone, just fantasising. I'd tell myself I would definitely not do it for real. Then my feelings turned to a certain smugness like a kid with a secret hideout in the bush that no one else knew about and then I would become somehow energised. Looking back, the energy state was the addictive thing.

Of course, my boyfriend Stu knew nothing. Before I walked into that house nearby with the dead woman, we lived a typically suburban life. No kids. We rented a small two-bedroom unit and like many people, dealt with the endlessness of bills and we both drove old shit-box cars. I wish that man had never pushed me into his house.

CHAPTER 3 VINCENT

FROM 2002 TO THE START OF 2007, I HAD NOT GIVEN a thought about that old lady's apparent suicide, rather I stored the memory away and life churned along as life does. Then, my rebellion against work and rules all spewed over into some kind of internal story with alternate ways of things to happen. A bit like those choose-your-own-adventure stories. My head tried out slightly different scenarios, with energy becoming the endpoint. Which storyline gave me the most energy? In real life, little details I would never have noticed a year ago, seemed to pop out at me.

The victim that appeared before my eyes at the start of my imaginations, had at that stage the face of a man named Vincent. Vincent, I am certain, ended the life of my best friend Debbie. She dated Vincent, a much older American psychiatrist in his late-forties that she met in the local supermarket of all places. In a short space of time, he wooed her heavily then pressured her to stay with him, sealing the deal with a diamond ring after seemingly exhausting himself with the effort. They were supposed to be married. She was supposed to be happy. Except they never did marry. She did not live long enough. And she never was happy.

His face, more typical of the over fifty, white Caucasian male, showed pudgy play-dough gibbets of flesh in his cheeks, jowl and neck. You could see the lumps just under his pasty, grey skin. This caused his small, beady, calculating eyes to recede right into his fat ugly head. You could tell that his body matched his face. Paunch from too much beer and flabby yuck everything. Not a toned fibre to be found anywhere. What amazes me is that even with such a disgraceful physique, he insisted on strutting around like he was back in his prime. Looking down his noses at everyone except others like him.

I guess you could say anger filled my thoughts in those early days whenever Vincent's face appeared in my head. Even Melita at the Fucktory noticed. She would say,

"If I could read auras, then yours would be bright red like a bushfire. What the hell are you so cross about this time?"

"Men!" I'd say as I slowly shoved a whole fallen apple pie with my steel-capped boot sideways across the concrete floor, Those grey-haired gits who get around like they own the world. That's what's pissing me off today.

I would tell her about this one that tried to cut me off in the car on the way to work or the bastard in the liquor shop who rushed to the counter to check his paunch producing wine through before me. Fact is, their faces all blended with each other to morph into one pasty, grey mass that looked like that useless psychiatrist Vincent. Everywhere I looked, there he was. Smug too. Each copy of Vincent that came along seemed smugger than the last. My anger built up. Melita and I discussed the power imbalances of our society and how people just accepted it all. Like the women we worked with. The helmet wenches had hearing loss, but they would laugh it off as a status symbol. Only people who had worked there a long time must have crap hearing so therefore they must be better than the rest, they reasoned. These people had become completely hoodwinked by the culture in the factory to the benefit of the owners. They lost their precious hearing and will probably have to wear costly hearing aids at an age much younger than most people. Except they will not be able to afford these devices because they never received enough pay. Or they'll be too proud to wear one and then become socially isolated and depressed and spiral down from there. All because, yes, they accepted their lot. Accept your lot in life. That is the Australian way. If you do not, you are a troublemaker or there is something wrong with you.

Whenever Melita and I talked about this stuff, for some reason, I kept linking my anger at what happened to Debbie to me. I must have accepted this to be fact. I failed so she died. Debbie died because her fiancé Vincent killed her. In 1998, he put the rope around her neck, I am sure of that and killed her. I should have tried so much harder to persuade her to leave him. If I had tried harder, I would still have my bestie to tell everything to. Not a sister but good as.

In addition, two parallel conversation topics kept running together for a few weeks. When Mel and I whinged about men, for me, all the men melded together to become Vincent. Such a ghastly name, but probably only due to my association with the horrible man. The other topic was about sticking to the rules and playing the game and how spineless it is to live your life like that. Not surprisingly I suppose, I merged the two topics into a theme of action whereby I would not let Vincent, nor all the merged Vincents, win. They will not continue living without punishment for not taking responsibility for their mistakes.

I would only need to see one instance of arrogance from a middle-aged man in the street and my mind would seethe. This emotion had to stop. To live like this is torture. I became tortured. To dampen down the whole thing, my imagined scenarios of Vincent's demise helped me. Instead of self-harm to ease the mental anguish, I found imagined harm to someone else worked, and you are left with no physical injury unlike the slice of a knife into one's delicate wrist. To me, those self-harm losers may as well, write it on their foreheads that they are not all right. Who wants other people to know that you are vulnerable and not in control? That is really putting yourself on the back foot, when it is a time to do the opposite. I hate to say it, but when you are weak it is precisely the time to do what you need to do, to cover up and appear stronger than what you might be feeling. I never understood cutting. Maybe, that's why I gained some degree of strength from scenarios of revenge and taking control of others instead of others taking control of me. I felt proactive to be 'doing something' even if it was not real. It gave me a kind of strength. I started to feel. Maybe, it's like an anorexic's mind structure where they perceive a world that they cannot control so they control one vital aspect that no one else can control for them, and that is the food items they put in their stomachs. That is their power, and they do all they can to retain it. Their secret actions of purging and exercise, tip over into pure obsessional behaviour and thus they are forever doomed unless the framework of their mind changes and they can pull out of the abyss and be normal again.

The scenarios I envisioned held parts that I felt in control of plus parts that surfaced from who knows where. Illogical unconscious segments gave them an uncontrolled unsettling flavour. However, it was these uncontrolled bits that remained as crucial rewards of excitement. The logical parts of taking out someone was like a chore and the other bits outside of me, were the reward and spice to feed me. Feeding me to keep me going.

To explain it more, I'd be thinking something like, right, how do I delete another waste-of-space Vincent from the world? I would have tried to take out the real one, but he moved to the USA. So, that's in the too hard basket. I discovered the joy of revenge scenarios on other replacement men. Excitement would abound when I thought of deftly pushing a knife through the skin, exposing the gristle underneath of that arrogant arsehole at the shops.

These scenarios would run in my head for a few days until they faded a bit, and I became bored and would introduce a degree of reality to it to make it more believable again. The realness would then fuel my energy levels. Realness and logic overruled, and I added the caveat to the question, how do I take out a waste of space Vincent… without being caught. To do that, I must be smart. That dead woman who apparently died from an overdose of prescription pethidine in the house up the road gave me my idea. What I did not understand at that time, was that it was really an idea of how to live, but to live in hell.

From what I have read from crime novels and seen in crime dramas on the television, people who kill more than once seem to kill in a similar way each time. For instance, creating a scene to appear like a break-and-enter, robbery or an accident. If I am careful and stage it like a suicide instead then that might work. That policeman was like; 'oh well, just another suicide. Let's just do the stuff we have to do and then that's that.' Unless something stands out to them, on site or whatever, why question a seemingly straightforward solution to their workday?

◊

In those days, I had these daydreams of harming people anywhere. In bed, driving the car, waiting out the back for a wave to appear on the horizon. Often a scenario set off inside me after an interaction or a flashback interaction with a Vincent-like man. At first, I'd be frustrated with hopelessness and then I started switching this over to empowering myself and thinking how I wielded power over them and the situation. I will be the one feeling smug thanks, not bloody you. Sounds super childish looking back, but that is how I felt.

These scenarios became quite intrusive to the point where it started to become, I would have to say, obsessive. I tried to turn the storylines back to something sweet, nice, and normal, but it wouldn't work. Naively, I believed that whenever I chose, I could go back to the way my thoughts once were. The powerful feeling became hard to give up. That is how it felt. That is how I looked at it.

Eventually the dark in me outweighed the light. I became weak in a sense because I succumbed to my thoughts. Initially the planning and preparation I made formed just another imaginary scenario. What was happening though, was I tried out different scenarios in my head to release the most excitement within me. For some reason, as I did this the men got younger and younger.

Eventually I hit on one scenario that just would not go away or morph into another. It would not shift from my mind. Nothing budged it. My descent into hell had begun. Alcohol gave me temporary relief. Drinking blocked the thoughts if I drank enough. Arguments started up with my boyfriend and he never knew what landscape my mind lived in. No one did. How great would it have been to talk to someone who felt like I did,

"Heh, what do you do in your spare time?"

"Oh, I relax by killing people off in my head."

"Yeah? Same here".

ó

One afternoon I ran across the grainy sand of Avoca Beach with my surfboard to enjoy a few waves with my surfing buddy Jess, with whom I got talking to one day when we were the only girls out on a big swell day. An unspoken line-up etiquette helped keep everyone at ease. Whoever missed the sets is permitted the next wave and we all paddled back out and wait our turn for the next wave to push through. As waves flowed in, people glided on and then one or two surfers who were last in line, would miss that set as the waves would lull again.

Unfortunately, along came a dickhead to wreck the ambience. Older than the other men, he stroked his way straight to the inside of the line-up, completely ignoring the stares of the two others whose turn it was. The first wave of the set loomed, and this useless bloke yelled, mine!

He took off on the turquoise wave breaking to the right. Okay, maybe he will work out what's happening as he paddles back out, I thought. We all know how hard it is to resist that first enticing wave but, nope, as soon as this guy reached the take-off zone again, he repeatedly paddled into the middle of the peak and muscled onto a wave. He did this with every single set, unsettling everyone.

This behaviour started to gnaw at me and before I knew it, my mind had unleashed an imaginary fury of punishment on this man. The scenario ran along surprisingly quickly in my head. The sun set and the beach darkened. The water became an inky black and the man finally had had enough. Following him to the car park, I put my board away in my car and grabbed my knife. Checking that the whole car park was empty and pitch black, I waited till he opened the back of his van and was putting his board in. Then I moved fast, as I saw him climb into the back of his van to push stuff forward. I was there, climbing in after him slicing into his side and then slamming the door hard behind me as I backed out. He wouldn't be taking another person's wave again.

Ô

This story ran through in my head in a flash and that somehow gave me some kind of strange strength. I crystallised my strength into action. Looking at the wave set coming and then looking at this man paddling directly from catching a wave to where this next right wave would peel, I propelled myself forward and round the back of him as fast as I could. I positioned myself with the right-of-way before he knew I was there. Then, as I stood up, I could see a flash of an image of the knife going into him in my mind's eye and I simultaneously yelled to him to get off! And he did!

Exhilarated by my newfound success, I prepared myself for another bout but annoyingly, he caught the next wave in. Either he became tired, thanks to all the waves he caught that the rest of us did not, or I'd like to think that he felt beaten. Beaten down by me. The pack would have gone back to its previous dynamics, except the school bell must have tolled and a bunch of hungry grommets, aka young kids, came out to also enjoy some fun. By the time Jess and I did go to shore, the selfish bloke had driven off. I did not think that much of it at the time. Gradually though these kinds of vicious scenarios started to surface like potholes all over my life. At first, I believed they helped me achieve things. My successful actions immediately after a nasty scenario seemed to convince me that violence, or at least violent thinking, is good and useful. If it is in my head, then I'm not hurting anyone. Why not exploit it? I did not hate that surfer because that sort of behaviour happens all the time. He annoyed me, yes, but not enough to end him. Who knows, he probably just experienced a hell day at work. Or maybe he gets beaten up by his missus and that's his only outlet so he can arrive home and be a loving father to his six kids or something.

○

This power strength dynamic really lodged inside me. I knew vaguely that I would have to do something dramatically different to move it out and on its way. I also felt disgusted with myself, as I felt a burgeoning excitement in acting out this scenario. The details became more elaborate as it had to catch up to the unconscious arousal side of the equation. Interestingly, the logical part veered off from the usual course of my storylines and took over, and a safe scenario presented itself. Gassing in a car might do. Just find someone.

That is the next dilemma. I had to find someone who deserves it. Vincent is and Vincents are everywhere. The more I thought about it, the more I brainwashed myself into thinking how I was doing everyone a favour subtracting scum from the earth. To hate an individual enough, my warped head produced the idea that my actions would help people.

CHAPTER 4 MELITA'S UNCLE

NIGHT SHIFT AT THE FACTORY AND MELITA AND I worked Line 7, the pocket pie conveyor belt.

"Ashli, my stomach feels so sore from all the pastry I just stuffed into my mouth at the oven", Melita said.

"Yeah, and you never get fat!" I replied. "Unlike some of those helmet heads around here."

The oven we loved. The hot, cooked pies moved out of the huge oven and onto the side arm conveyor, to be sent along for packing into boxes. They sometimes jammed up against each other. This caused the edges to break. If a real stuff up happened and one was not adept at spacing them safely for their next leg of the journey, they piled up and failed to move along until some fell on the floor. We'd regularly lift a few off the jamming zone, to cool at the side, readying them for eating. Plate-sized big pies broke up and misbehaved, squashing each other more readily than the small ones. This meant our stomachs benefited more on those days, but take-homes were harder to snaffle, given the larger size compared to the pocket pies.

Our bellies full, Melita and I talked. "Do you know anyone who has suicided Mel?" I asked.

"Yeah, me uncle. He tried a few times before he finally did

it."

"How? Is that okay if I ask you that?"

"Sure. He and I weren't close. I only saw him every few years when he came down from Brisbane on his way to Melbourne to visit his mother. He'd arrive late, stay overnight and be gone before dawn."

"What did he do?"

"The stuff he tried before he finally got there was slicing his legs up. He ended up in hospital and had to have heaps of stiches. That left him with all these scars, and he always wore long pants after that. Later on, he jumped off a bridge into a river wearing a backpack full of rocks. That failed too and he swam ashore. Finally, he gassed himself in his garage. Left the engine running with a hose stuck in the exhaust pipe. A neighbour found him but way too late."

"Did he actually admit to cutting up his legs himself?"

"Yeah, later when he woke up after surgery and mum said he felt all ashamed about it."

"Did anyone think someone else may have attacked him or anything like before he woke up?"

"Nope, not that I know of."

"Did he leave a note or anything?"

"Nah, until then no one even knew he was even depressed except his doctor."

"I wonder how they knew he did it deliberately then, and not someone else doing it to him?"

"Dunno really. Never thought about it."

Driving home after the shift ended, I thought about all the techniques people used to kill themselves, gassing, hanging, stabbing, jumping off things, shooting, overdosing. Then I thought about how, even in, what seemed to me, an unusual case of attempted suicide such as Melita's uncle, no one seemed to question that attempted suicide occurred rather than attempted homicide. Surprising I felt, especially given that not many people slash up their own bodies as a way of topping themselves. I can understand the lack of questioning for the gassing though. That's typically a suicide technique. Plus he had a history of attempts.

As I drove along, I barely noticed the train moving parallel with me heading towards Woy Woy. Glancing up at it, I could see people's heads inside, I thought of another suicide method right there, of how suiciders sometimes lie down on the tracks or jump off a platform in front of a train. My next thought turned to the question of how to make someone do it. How to do that and not be seen. Night, drugs and dragging. So many methods to contemplate. Even though I felt tired from working the twelve-hour shift on my feet at the fucktory, a wave of excitement started to wash through me giving me a sort of a hit from head to toe. I could see the possibilities stretch out before me of manipulating different ways of suicide to have situations appear. Situations that convey suicide, only they are not. Immediately after those thoughts, I could feel a plan starting.

CHAPTER 5 DEBBIE

DEBBIE AND I BECAME BEST FRIENDS AND WE
lived as flatmates years ago. She was fun and outgoing.
Boyfriends came and went. She maintained her identity and
remained pretty much herself while dating them all. She
confided in me about all her dates until Vincent came along. He
changed her and it was immediate. He differed to the others in
that he seemed to be some type of father figure to her. All
conservative and super straight but super charming. His
personality fit that of the older Australian baby boomer
generation man and yet he was only in his late forties. Way old
for her too. He smothered her with undivided attention then
shackled her to him with that fugly, diamond engagement ring.

Prior to her moving into Vincent's plush waterfront residence,
Debbie and I enjoyed living together. She was the first person
to treat me with no judgement when it seemed the rest of the
world treated me like crap. Exclusion at school, no siblings and
no friends shunted me to outsider status. Like a fear-biting pup,

I think I pushed people away first before they pushed me away. Debbie and I had no mutual contacts, so she had no preconceived negative ideas about me when I answered her advertisement for a flatmate. Because I sensed her to be a kind and non-threatening type of person, and I felt relaxed around her, it was easy for me to be soft and get along with her. I recognised a vulnerability and naïveté in Debbie that reminded me of how I used to be. This made me protective of her because I always felt she was weak whereas I had overcome my weakness and become strong. I could feel both frustration and envy when people did the wrong thing by her and take advantage, she might show annoyance at them but never anger. She is the only person in my life I ever trusted. I don't have siblings, and Debbie was to me not just a best friend but a sister. If I'd had a brother or sister, I would have been fiercely loyal and protective of them, I'm sure of it.

∾

With persistent coaxing, I persuaded her to get a tattoo with me. We chose a simple figure of eight, black eternity, lemniscate symbol sealing our friendship forever. Often, we'd touch these together in times of solidarity and break into fits of laughter because hers was positioned on her right ankle and mine on my left bicep.

At night, we'd lie on my bed talking till the wee hours discussing everything and anything. Debbie had a way of saying stuff in such an innocent and goofy way that I often cracked up laughing. Wanting her to be happy, I made a big effort not to be overly critical of her charismatic and ugly new man. Our friendship meant too much to me to risk losing her so I bit my tongue more times than she would ever know. Sometimes I'd be snarky about him, and she'd interpret this as possessiveness. This instigated arguments but despite this we'd always make up and remain friends. I felt it was too hard to talk properly with her about him and I think that's why she never confided in me completely about what he was really like with her. Especially after she moved in with him. All I know is after that ring padlocked her to him, she started to become very unhappy, and I failed to help her. If I tried too hard, I'd lose my best friend, so I became selfish and I left her to him. I didn't try hard enough.

ↄ

Of course, Vincent didn't approve of me. He thought he could hide that from me until one time I was having a go at him at their place about something. I don't remember what but significantly, it was in front of Debbie. Debbie left to go and fetch Vincent more beer from the refrigerator in the garage and then suddenly, Vincent had me in a tight headlock, spitting in my ear, that I should 'shut the fuck up or else', his vile acrid smelling breath sucking up the oxygen in the air. He thought I was a bad influence on Debbie. Wrong and wrong. He's the bad influence on her. Too shocked to say anything, I kept forever silent. As her friend, I had to remain loyal. To be loyal, I needed to be supportive of her decisions in life as hard as that is. I was there, ready to listen to her complaining and debriefing of her life with Vincent except she wouldn't, and it didn't help our relationship when I finally directly tried to persuade her to ditch him. What started to happen though, as Vincent became increasingly controlling, jealous and then physically harmful towards Debbie, I became more and more protective of her and of course, angry at him. My anger upset her, so I started to repress it. I concealed it to protect her.

She'd confided in me a few times how she grew up in an argumentative, combative family and her way to avoid the social stress was to become insignificant and let her older sisters cop the wrath when they argued with her dad. I think that may be why Vincent drew out the same mousey behaviour in her. It also meant she couldn't handle my burgeoning fury.

⚬

Vincent's attitude affected me in a way that I started to notice his bad attributes in men all over the place. I globalised it. Drop in, dick shits out in the surf, arrogant drivers in their muscle cars aggressively cutting me off when I'm just trying to smoothly merge, patronising policemen giving me unjust tickets, all started to really make me angry. An important aspect to this I also observed, is how other women just sucked up this sort of shit. Doing nothing. Doormats. This grated on me.

I shouldn't have allowed myself to even notice these types of men at all. They've always been around and always will be. They are not worth worrying about. The reality is there are enough normal, kind-hearted, and genuine men in the world who are the complete antithesis of them. In fact, there are probably many more compassionate ones who adore women and have immense respect for them than the women despisers who treat us like crap. I wasn't noticing these good ones. If I had, like I used to, I may have kept balanced, normal and everything would have been okay. But it's like I was a racehorse with the blinkers on. Gradually I became unbalanced and severely out of kilter. Then the postie came by with the mail.

CHAPTER 6 DAVE

HOW DO PEOPLE FEEL DEEP WITHIN THEIR CORE
when they take absolute control of another person's life? Today
is the day. I have prepared and I will be exhilarated. They were
my thoughts on that otherwise typical spring day in 2007. A day
forever permeated by the smell of peppermint and wet
eucalyptus.

o

The day is now. My hope is that I will feel something. I drive
across to the neighbouring suburb that borders the bush and is
at the far end of the beach near where I live. I park in a small car
park, nose out ready for a quick exit. I lock up and walk back
home along the beach. Once home, I pack a floral-patterned tote
bag with my recent purchases, the receipt for the cash I paid for
the pipe, a small towel and my favourite knife. My head throbs
with a headache, so I dose up with some paracetamol. A packet
of codeine fortified paracetamol in the form of Panadol Forte
positioned next to the Panadol catches my eye. I slide some
tablets out of the foil, walk to the kitchen and crush them under

32

a cup. The powder I funnel into a snap lock bag and I put that into the tote bag. Last things into the bag are car keys and a change of clothes. The receipt bugs me, so I pull it out and stare at it. The date is at the top, so I carefully rip that bit off.

Just before 6pm, I change into a dress and grab a cardigan. As I run my lipstick along my lips the realness of the situation almost penetrates but I restrain my thoughts and manage to block it. It's as if I hold up a large medieval shield in front of me as a force field. The details of the environment around me stop registering. I can smell no external smells like the cooking aromas from next door, nor sounds such as distant traffic. Those smells and sounds are distracting and make the present real. Without them, I exist in an unreal, fake state. Locking the heavy door behind me, I start my detached walk to the nearby skate ramp.

○

Leaning back nonchalantly on a sandstone rock at the park is the Postie. Seeing me, he walks towards me in his cheap, drab clothes and we climb into his car. I fake my attraction to my fake Vincent and together we drive across the suburb, almost right past my car and into the nearby National Park. We stroll amongst the grove where the big red Waratah flowers live. I have stuffed up. The waratahs have finished flowering and there are no blooms in amongst the green shrubbery at all. Luckily, the man is not at all perturbed. I guess he is not going to be. He is there for other unspoken reasons. I suggest we walk to a nearby lookout to see the beautiful, big and majestic Hawkesbury River. My goal being to drag our putrid time out until the cover of dark. We ooh and aah as the sun sets in a clear strip of sky under a thick wad of heavy cloud cover. Thankfully, the filth-ball has not made any moves on me yet. We stand above a cliff with no guard rail and thoughts ambush my mind of running hard and pushing him off, but that scenario I hadn't prepared for, and I don't want to be caught. We see no one else, as the weather is overcast and spitting raindrops on and off. By the time we reach the car, it starts to rain properly, and the evening becomes dark. The smell of wet eucalyptus permeates the thick air. Dave, he told me his name as we left the skate park, sits still in the driver's seat. I notice a slight minty menthol odour.

"You stay there while I get you a drink." I say to him.

"You don't mind bourbon, do you?"

"Gees, you've got drinks!"

"I come prepared" I say.

"Well then yeah, I'll go a bourbon. Sure."

I'm thinking, 'yeah, I bet. You probably are one of those fucked up losers who drink anything provided it contains alcohol.'

Down low behind his seat, I hold a can in my bag while I open it and tip the Panadol Forte powder into it. I swirl it round and round to try and mix it. Shaking it a bit, I nearly slosh it all in my bag. I squeeze between the seats and lower myself in the front next to him, handing him the doctored drink. After just half the can he starts talking shit. All about his woeful bloody life. On and on. Sad and depressed he seems to me. You'd think it would take more than half a bloody can to reach that point of spilling your guts about your sorrowful lot in life. I ask him if he's received any kind of help at all and he says antidepressants are a waste of money. Its money that he never has because he feeds the pokies with all his dough. I can't believe this idiot is spilling all his pathetic crap out to me. Little does he know; I am the last person who would give a shit. The more he talks though, the more he does not fit the Vincent I've been wanting to get out of my head and annihilate. There is no way Dr Vincent would disclose any of his weaknesses like this. I feel my resolve receding. But then, the amorous side of the bloke emerges, and he forgets his shit life and becomes arrogant and sleazy.

"Enough about me, let's get into business here", he demands with a tacky, greasy wink of the eye.

He starts undressing, taking off his jacket. That fits with Vincent again. I start to suspect my heart rate is rising. At least I'm hoping it is. I tell him to stay in his seat while I fix another drink. Then he says maybe he should be worried about being over the alcohol limit. I reassure him and say we can go for a walk after and by the time he drives, he'll be well under. With those words, I internally giggle because I'm thinking that the next time, he's in a proper car, it'll be a hearse. The rain pelts down heavier now, and I open my door and rush to the back door. I leap into the backseat and slide behind him slamming the door to stop the wet. As I pretend to fuss in the bag, a wave of unreality sweeps over me. My hands feel and fondle the cold soft, nylon belt. I wrap a towel a few times around it to make the width as wide as possible to leave no impressions later. My heart really does pound in my chest, and I look at Vincent's face in the revision mirror. I stand up a bit holding the towel belt thing in both hands and then fast in one movement, I flop it over his head and pull both ends as hard as I can against the chair. His hands fly up to pull it off, but I use all my weight and leverage to lean back and keep up the tension around his ugly throat. This goes on for a bit and then, suddenly, the struggle ends, and he goes kind of all dangly. I still hold on hard some more, thinking that maybe he is playing dead. Then I let go and he just stays there completely still. Looking in the mirror I can see his eyes bulging out a bit and his pupils look wrong somehow. I can't stop taking in the look of his face. I'm not sure how long I stay staring.

Smoothly and without panic, I move into the next phase of my preparations. I pull out a garbage bag and place the towel and belt in it. Then I slide on the gloves and take the hose pipe and garden hose from the bag and climb out into the rain. The new hose pipe is stiff and is almost the same diameter as the exhaust pipe. I'm having a huge fight with it trying to get it over and around. The exhaust pipe is wider than I'd expected. I hadn't even thought about different cars having different sized exhaust pipes and I curse myself because I had failed to properly think through this part. I manage to force the rubber a few inches along. I put the green garden hose in and then start wrapping the tape around. It's all getting wet from the rain and not sticking together tight. I try to dry it all with a towel which works. After winding down dead Dave's window a bit, I thread the pipe in, then from the back seat I wind the window up to jam it and thrust his jacket into the space left above the glass. With a second thought, I pull the jacket through the window and put that into my backpack. He is not in need of that now and it's a waste of a good jacket, I decided.

The rain is great for deterring anyone coming out to walk in the bush or look at the river view. To fill the air space of the open window, I calmly walk around to the passenger door and pull and tug at the car seat cover. Once that's off the seat, I walk back to the door behind the driver's door, climb back in a bit and push it into the space from the inside. My arm touches his face. This is a dead body now. The body is warm like it's still alive. My fingers push into his flabby cheek. I can't really explain why I do what I did next. I reached back to my backpack and pulled out a small red penknife, my Swiss army knife, from a small, meshed compartment inside. Walking over to the driver's seat, I fold out the sharp blade. I fold back the shirt sleeve on the arm nearest me to expose the hairy bicep. Where it bulges, I slice into the flesh but only making a tiny centimetre incision. Some blood comes out. Blood comes out and looks alive, but it is not alive, its dead blood. I cover the mark with the sleeve and go and wipe the blood on the blade onto a brown leaf I pick up from the ground wiping it with an alcohol wipe and folding it back together again.

Urgency then prevails over fascination, and I take the alcohol wipes and wipe down every surface I had touched, both in the back and the front. The wipes go into a freezer bag and into the backpack. Power over absolutely everything is what I am feeling right now. It is a non-tangible thing no one else can understand but me. This is mine. I grab my bag and reprimand myself for not considering the weather with my packing as I will soon become drenched. Then I wipe the outside door handles, reach in for the keys, place them in the ignition and turn the fucker on. The handbrake is already on. Just before I switch off the internal cabin light, I peer into his face and absorb the whole dead body presence. I don't understand why but I want to take a piece of what I'd done with me. Illogical really. That's the jacket I suppose. Looking down at his crotch, I see his fake leather belt is adorned with a silver buckle. Pushing him forward in the seat, I pull his belt through the loops in his jeans and free it from his body. I push his body back and stuff the belt into my backpack. I feel a hot feeling of inner strength and paradoxically numbness and detachment. Looking at his face, it is Dave's face though and no longer Vincent's face. I switch off the light, shut the door quietly and take my bag back down the track towards the lookout. Then I run.

After about ten minutes of adrenalin-fuelled exhilarating running, I stop under a sandstone ledge and change my clothes into a black tracksuit and black sandshoes. The tracksuit top has a hood which I position over my head. The garbage bag I check, and I feel the belt. I'd forgotten to pack a torch as well as the raincoat, so I feel around for my knife with my fingers. Down on the dirt in front of me, I raggedly cut off some of the fake black leather belt at the end where the silver buckle is attached. I place the buckle in my pocket and the rest of that belt back in the bag with the nylon struggle belt and it was then that I remembered I'd forgotten to leave behind the receipt for the hose. That's four stuff ups. No raincoat, hose that's not adjustable enough, no torch and then forgetting the placement of the receipt. Points to remember.

I set off for the lookout where I throw the garbage out into black space as far as I can. Then, I pelt back along the track to another track down to Pearl beach, a neighbouring beach to where my car is parked. Rushing down the hill through the bush, I slip and fall over a few times and hardly feel a thing. I quickly walk through the streets to the beach and slow my speed down to look casual. I don't expect any busybody eyes on such a dark rainy night as this but just in case, I walk confidently along the beach and up onto the rock shelf track that leads around the waters' edge to the next beach. Here I find my car and I climb in still feeling sky high from what I'd just actually achieved. Driving back home, I begin to have thoughts that the whole deal is surreal and that I had not done anything. Back in the house though, after a hot steaming shower, I reached into the soaked floral bag and immediately my hand touched the cold metal buckle. I recoiled as shock floods through me. It's like a charge is pulsing through the metal to my hand with the touch of someone else's belonging. I strut into the kitchen and search for a plastic clip container. I place the buckle belt bit in a tea towel, and then stash it behind my shoes in my wardrobe. Later, I will decide where to hide it properly. The buckle is like some kind of memento I guess to look at and hold. The jacket is mine to wear. It has the damp odour from the night. One of the pockets has a small mouth freshener pump spray. That's the smell in Dave's car.

During the coming days, the inner strength returns then wanes and then takes over my thoughts. When the energy dissipates, I slip the unwashed jacket on and wear it. It's like a cloak from the enemy feeding me their power. Replenishing my strength before the next kill. Stupid but true.

CHAPTER 7 FEELING

EMOTIONALLY I FELT INTENSE YET MIXED
feelings the days and months after that death. My mind jumped
around between feeling good and bad, sad and bad, scared and
ashamed and then triumphant and feeling wholly alive. At the
back of my mind, I knew there was absolutely no relief because
there had been no action against Vincent. However, I had
managed to demonstrate how easy it is to make a murder
appear as a suicide. That's what Vincent had done. He killed
Debbie and blamed it on her frail mind. He got away with
murder by saying Debbie's death was suicide. It is too easy to
make homicide look like suicide. This is what people need to
know. It's not out there as common knowledge. There must be
stacks of people who do this, and no one knows. The worst bit
is the victim's family who become fuckups forever because
they believe whoever it was that they loved, just up and
abandoned them when in fact that's a crock because some
dickhead went and killed them. They live a tortured life from
lies. Do the cops care? Some but not enough of them. The few
decent officers that do find a case that becomes stuck to their
ribs and they genuinely and attempt to pursue the truth, I'd
imagine become stifled by their peers' laziness, barriers of red

tape, lack of resources plus lack of support and recognition from their supervisors.

It's a lot easier to put an unnatural death to bed by labelling it as suicide than going up against all the walls and investigating those variables that may be manipulated by another party. For instance, even when ambiguous variables do surface as potentially suspicious, the New South Wales standard police questionnaire requires no sticky questions to be asked of next of kin. In Australia anyway there are not enough assumed suicides that turn out to be homicides to warrant any form of standardised interrogation of relatives and family to reveal concocted 'suicide' indicators. Unfortunately, the one high profile case that might have highlighted this is perhaps paradoxically actually a suicide. Caroline Byrne was found at the bottom of the notorious suicide site of The Gap in Sydney. Her fiancé ended up in the slammer until acquitted a few years later. Caroline's body was found nine metres from the cliff base which meant people thought she had been being picked up and 'spear thrown' out and off the cliff by someone. She had all the significant risk factors for a suicidal person, especially having attempted it previously but it is illogical to think that someone would bother with lifting her high up above their head and throwing her far out. It's risky throwing a heavy cumbersome weight because the thrower might end up accidentally going over too from the momentum. What would be plausible is if someone did push her off the cliff, they would have only needed to force her just over the edge to achieve their goal. It also looks more authentic as a suicide to simply drop someone over the edge because that's how people expect most suicidal people to carry out their end-of-life jump. Suicide jumpers sometimes leap right out into space in a huge head-first dive, like from a swimming pool diving board. The tests done for the court case against Caroline's partner, perhaps failed, because the forensic scientist didn't consider the topography of the cliff in the tests. There was one just like that at Terrigal years ago. Think also of the 9-11 leapers. Plus, I know for a fact that it is possible to fly out a long way into space with a run-up, providing you have enough height underneath you. I say this because once as a school kid, during swimming classes, the teacher said we could jump off the five-metre-high diving platform into the pool. This was on the condition that we stepped off and didn't run and jump out. If any of us ran, then the whole class would be made to get out of the pool. So, on this particular day, when I thought the teacher's head was turned away, I ran three steps only, then launched into the air, headfirst, arms stretched as far as I could out into space. I landed almost in the shallow part of the pool. Three strong strides were all it took me to fly out in a horizontal arc to hit the water about twelve meters away from the end of the platform. The teacher saw me and that ended the class's fun. I had managed an excessively long jump, like flying. Because of my disobedience all the kids were ordered out of the pool and everyone, especially the boys, whinged at me as they climbed out to go and change.

The teacher's misunderstanding was she thought I cared about what the other classmates thought of me. Because I didn't, her punishment was no deterrent.

6

People misunderstanding me became a common thread in my life. Probably my fault for falsely mimicking other peoples' behaviours to obtain certain responses back from them. So, in effect I controlled their vision and assumptions about me, or so I felt. No way would anyone really discover the real me. That's because no one would understand the real me. Growing up there were issues constantly revolving about right or wrong. How do you explain that 'yeah, I know such and such that I did is wrong, but hey, I just don't care? I can't help it'.

"But what you did, hurt someone and how would you like that done to you? Can't you see how that would hurt them, Ashli?" they'd whine.

Well in fact I can imagine what that would feel like if it was done to me and that's kind of why I did it, or at least, I know and I don't care, full stop. Yes, my parents struggled with me and so did the dumb teachers.

I look at people who blubber and cry at life's inequities and I class them as fools. Get a grip. Too much energy is wasted worrying about everyone else in this world. One thing that maybe makes me different to a psychopath is that people with that personality type are said to lack empathy. I don't lack empathy. At least if I'm interpreting empathy correctly. I can imagine the anguish and grief someone might experience when seeing their beloved dog becoming flattened under the tires of, say, a dump truck. Sometimes I can understand what it would be like to be those six drivers stuck behind me who are very frustrated and angry at me. Them beeping their horns and making a huge racket because I'm not turning left with the traffic but waiting till I can cross all three lanes of traffic at once so I can make a quick turn right a few meters later and avoid driving the long way. I get that and I don't care. I can imagine what people are feeling but not really feel myself. What this means is that I can be extremely patient when it comes to other people's actions on occasion. I will think to myself, 'nah don't get worked up' and sometimes, 'good on them for breaking the mould and doing something out of the ordinary'. Around them there might be people harping on about how it is wrong and not the etiquette but here finally is someone who tells them to stick it, not necessarily with words but through their actions. Rules are usually created to fit a generalised situation. Take traffic lights. Designed for high to medium traffic flow of vehicles and pedestrians. They are ineffective when there are low flows of traffic like when you might be driving along at 2 am and stop at a red light but no one is in sight so what is the point in hanging there wasting time. Society is overboard with rules and anyone who adheres to it all is truly brainwashed. That's not hard though with the way our society rears their young to accept all the propaganda about how to live your life all proper.

6

No mention of Dave's death appeared in the news. He probably just needed a helping hand anyway given his sorry story. My new problem now became my new outlook of life's little enjoyments. Instead of relishing a beautifully cooked roast pork dinner or relaxing in the sun thinking absent thoughts at the beach, the little stuff seemed of no consequence, and I failed to enjoy any of it anymore. Considering the gigantic act that I actually did that rainy night, the small stuff of life became even smaller. I imagine this is a bit like a drug addict's life where living revolves around the next hit and other enjoyments no longer rate. The void became full to the brim of obsessive thoughts about that night. I replayed the whole trip, not just the moment of death but all the other details. This made me feel alive. I knew it to be bad, but it became all-consuming and the more I thought about it, the more I felt excited and the more I didn't care. I kept returning to the realisation that our lives are full of constraints that are not always of our choosing. That's only if we choose to let others rule what we think, what we do, how we do things. We will all die and why live bound by other human's lines in the sand. Cultural and social constructs bind and control our petty lives. We can all break free, but it takes guts. It's my inner balance that I know I must act for and not anyone else's. The trick is maintaining the inner drives that are deviant to society's parameters but in a sustainable way. In other words, not getting caught. If you are busted, you potentially become constrained and bound up in a 3D box. It is fine to just imagine non-conventional thoughts and play it all out in the head but that is not truly nourishing one's inner core or inner being. Again, feeding that inner balance requires careful thought to keep it all running into the future.

During those first months after Dave, when I felt frazzled, annoyed, bored even, a brief visit to the car park helped me out. It put me back in control again. I tried not to go but I couldn't resist the compulsion to relive. Sometimes I'd go just to feel something. Usually, I'd just drive in when it was dark like that night, and no one would be around to get in the way of my thoughts. Parking opposite where Dave's car was, I'd sit there facing the empty car spot in my old Barina just absorbing it in. Then, I'd get out and walk over to the car space and stand next to the now gone car and replay the words said and the exact actions that happened. I'd relive the whole scenario that happened in my mind. The second time I visited I'd taken the silver belt buckle with me, to feel the smooth steel in my pocket while right there again. This made it extra real and heightened my whole reliving experience.

If people were around, I'd walk down the dark track I'd taken that night. I'd walk for a bit and then head off the track into the thick scrub. This region beyond the car park is covered in sandstone boulders amongst spiky heath and I'd climb through it all until I'd find a flat rock where I could sit down. If someone had walked down the path, they would not know I was there at all.

Later if no one was around when I drove in, I'd park my car in the same spot as Dave did and I'd climb in the back behind the driver's seat. I didn't bother with the walk. One time, to really relive that night, I took Dave's jacket for the smell but later I just took the mouth freshener spray bottle and sprayed it on the back of the front seat.

◊

At some point during my descent into hell I'd created some complex bad associations. Knowing what I know now, you can change these associations, but it's taken me a long time to find this out. In other words, fantasies, or fetishes or whatever you call them, are fluid and interchangeable. If there's a shift once, there can be a shift twice and many more times. We do not need to be slaves to our minds. Hard to know this when so many variables together 'reward' us for a certain behaviour. I wonder now if I worked in a different job and was busy completing fulfilling projects and not felt bored with it all, then maybe I would not have chosen these other 'projects' instead. Why did I fill the holes in my life with these kinds of missions?

Even now, nearly two decades later, I'm underwater looking up through brown-grey murkiness at the surface confused and trying as hard as I can to figure out where exactly I am and how the bejesus I got here. I'm hoping I'll burst through and up and life will become clear again and beautiful and colourful. And I'll be happy. All of that. I want to be able to take a breath of healthy, oxygenated air. I keep trying to reach the surface but never seem to break through. People who write autobiographies sometimes say writing is cathartic. Writing this hell crap of mine is harder than anything. Maybe when we write, THE END we are finally released. Hope so. That's what is pulling me along right at this moment. I must keep going to remove this dark wretched pain deep inside me.

CHAPTER 8 DENIAL

TIME AMBLED ALONG. AS I WENT THROUGH THE everyday motions of life, I would find myself working on the details of stopping Vincent from hurting anyone else. This time it will work. I will succeed and then I can stop. This one is the last one. All these thoughts are excruciating and exhilarating. Guilt and shame but equally strength and energy. Torment. Denial helped. The denial of the whole thing. Denial that I did what I did to Dave, denial that I felt what I felt. I could pretend nothing ever actually happened and I lucid dreamed the whole thing. I managed this for weeks at a stretch. Then my carefully made mental slip knots around my mind restraining me would begin to loosen. Walking through Erina Fair, the local bustling shopping plaza, I'd find myself fondling a silver belt buckle in a clothing shop, and I'd be immersed into a completely noiseless void, far from the shoppers around me. Or the smell of big raindrops penetrating the dry parched dirt in the backyard at home near the back step, might send me instantly back to when I walked away from the dirt car park that night.

Crucially, denial invaded my perception of Vincent. And I let it. This is the crux of my flawed psyche and the depth of my weakness. They say people who are violent are cowards. Well, that's me. Like handing over hard-earned cash on Melbourne Cup Day for a pointless waste of money bet you know wont magically convert your life into shiny and new, but you submit to your stupid feelings of possibility anyway. You want the white, red rush of adrenaline even if it's just for a few seconds. You know it makes you feel alive.

I've tried to untangle why I sent myself down this path of destruction and I have come up with what I think is true. Vincent repeatedly hurt Debbie, and I continually failed to stop him. There were so many bruises hidden under her sleeves. Purple circles from finger depressions and big broad yellow blotches. Twice I saw some marks encircling her neck. He was nice as pie to her when I saw them together. Announcing to people, even the random service station attendant, how much he adores her and how proud he is of his gorgeous girlfriend. He eventually killed her, and I failed to stop him. To rid myself of my overwhelming guilt (however irrational this is) of his final act of destroying her, I tell myself in a hazy, half seen way that redemption is possible, and I can be free of guilt but only if I can prevent him from hurting anyone else. The denial is my act of replacing innocent men with Vincent. They become Vincent. Dave stopped means Vincent is stopped. The guilt should have stopped. It didn't. Another dimension of guilt replaced it.

Another layer is that I recognise that I am striving to show the world how easily Vincent evaded suspicion with his technique of staging Debbie's death as a suicide. I want to blow him and anyone else who does this, out of the water. That is my driver behind the modes I choose. Irrational because I can't let on to the 'world' what I'm doing. The world will never know if I never am caught. I must also be in denial to not realise by doing this then I am as bad as Vincent and all the rest of them! And worse! That's the only explanation I can come up with. Maybe I keep ludicrously telling myself, I'm doing good by these actions. I don't know.

6

When I'm having doubts and I am really trying hard to bury the whole thing, I provoke the man subtly to illicit a shit response from him. Then I can seamlessly transform him back into either Vincent or at that specific time, into all the chauvinistic woman-hating pigs that I need to insanely 'protect' people from. Only by provoking him can I summon my power and anger to continue carrying out my plan with him.

CHAPTER 9 BRIDGES AND CLIFFS

MY MUNDANE WORK IN THE FUCKTORY ALLOWED my mind to inhabit my other world. The rhythm of the machines clunking monotonously lulled me into my fantasies. This is where the bulk of my fantastic ideas, where once that's all they were, became crystallised into real life or rather, real death. As the warm pocket pies rode the conveyor belt and I'd push four into a fresh box, my plans would develop. Now and then, my concentration slipped, and a berry pie landed on the unforgiving concrete floor, breaking up into pieces with a squishy red mass oozing out. Red, like blood.

First, I'd run through scenarios of the different ways of staging suicides but without any places in mind. It felt scattered and precarious somehow. Injecting a specific location grounded it. The main components I planned were a location, staging the scene to look like a suicide and the fatal method I'd inflict. Another factor too was how to lure a person to the location.

With Dave, I don't know if I was just lucky with how well that panned out or not. I did identify some blunders. Getting caught was not my aim, so precautions and planning became key. To ensure success I carried out reconnaissance trips to various potential sites. Attractive site attributes for outdoor suicides included lack of people, remote but close enough for me to exit in a short span of time, easy access and somewhere with plausible cover. When I say plausible cover, I mean the site needs to be a place with commonplace human activities carried out there so that I can adopt them and blend into the environment with no suspicion at all. The plausible cover must extend to include a place that I can convince a stranger to go to with me under the guise of some typical lifestyle type activity. Lastly, and most importantly, there must be scope for a convincing cover for me to leave the scene after the act is complete. Ideally, no one will lay eyes on me, and precaution is priority if I am to succeed in my new 'venture'.

A well-used site is the Mooney Mooney Bridge, spanning an under fit, brackish creek just south of the Gosford turnoff on the freeway. Historically, many people chose that bridge to end their lives since its construction decades ago. Maybe it was attractive because it was publicised in the media as higher than the Harbour Bridge. No coming back from that height. Word of mouth can be powerful too with copycat suicides favouring that bridge. The strong link to suicide made me visit it. Driving over the six-lane bridge, I'd never noticed the details of the fence, so I had to take a closer look.

One afternoon, I drove up to the freeway and drove as slow as I could over the bridge in the left lane. That fence was high, but the southern end looked like people could scramble over where it ended. I kept driving up the hill and turned off the freeway at the Peats Ridge turnoff. There I joined the old Pacific Highway which took me back towards the bridge where I turned off onto a dirt track running parallel to the narrow creek. As I drove, I couldn't get around the problem of trying to get someone over that steel fence because it loomed up so high above the road. They would have to be dead too so that meant I'd need another location for that. Also, it was a main road and although in the early hours of the morning maybe there would be little traffic, all I needed was one nocturnal truck driver to see me struggling with a corpse and that would be it for me.

Underneath the bridge, I drove along the gravelly track and

under the enormous and imposing arcs of concrete that support the vast bridge. I opened my driver's window and heard the rumble of traffic right up above. It was a scummy kind of place. Rubbish strewn around. Toilet paper, weeds. A depressing vibe for all the suicides that have happened right at this exact location. I stopped the car near the edge of the creek and got out of the car. No one was around. I looked up at the bridge and imagined the people straddling the fence and then falling from the sky. I expected it would look a bit like what people witnessed during 9/11 when people escaped the burning towers by leaping off and into the sky. The difference was those particular people wanted to live not die. Maybe some of these people who suicided right here, also did not really want to die. They simply felt trapped, and this was their last desperate act for some form of release.

I looked up again at the fence that framed the road across the bridge. The fence had been modified so it no longer became an easy option for jumping people as the guard fence is now much higher than before with vertical bars and a concave shape at the top specifically designed to prevent people climbing over. Even when standing on the roof of a parked car it would be difficult. Still maybe somewhere down below could work if I could figure out a different suicide method to stage. It's a good site for the suicide staging using exhaust but I needed to find a different suicide method to complete my next example of homicidal suicide staging or *huicide*. Also, a single-entry road is not so good if someone happened to drive in when I drove out and they notice me leaving. Still, it felt like a perfect suicide place. Under the bridge feels lonely because there are the sounds of busy people, the rest of the world up top, driving across the bridge uncaring of the lonely person underneath looking up towards them. Physically these people are so close to the lonely soul below, but galaxies away as they are all complete strangers who are not at all connected or concerned about the one below who is about to annihilate themselves to oblivion. I can understand how someone could feel abandoned by the world down under the dark shadow of that bridge.

6

In amongst the rubbish strewn by the creek felt like a good drug dealing venue which got me thinking about someone overdosing. Problem with that is I don't know how to get the drugs. Or how to even use them convincingly. Plus, I'd have to have other signs that differentiate the death as suicide, not as an overdose mistake. I couldn't work out how to convince someone to drive there and meet me at night either. It's too far to get out there on foot.

Driving out of and away from that eerie space I realised how useful reconnaissance trips were to really nut out what can and can't work. Although I felt disappointed the site didn't seem suitable, I had progressed with my project.

6

Another popular site for jumping to your death is the Central Coast's equivalent to Sydney's The Gap, which is The Skillion at Terrigal. I assessed this site too. Merited with its undeveloped low barriers, lack of surveillance and strong sheer cliff face, the downside is two barriers before the edge that make for difficulties encouraging someone to straddle over those. Also, the escape route for me is rather claustrophobic with only a one-way exposed road out. However, I did notice it to be an ideal spot to dump.

CHAPTER 10 GLINDA

THERE IS A GNAWING FEELING INSIDE MY HEAD. A bit like one of those persistent headaches at the back near the neck that just niggles and won't leave you alone, except there is no actual pain. The gnawing is distracting me. I really cannot concentrate on things. I feel scattered and can't focus on one thing. I suspect there is a fight going on between Glinda and Evillene. Glinda is blocking Evillene. At least she is trying to. Whenever the urge to kill surfaces, Glinda pushes it away and tries to detach. In detaching, normal day to day actions are not quite executed smoothly. Stuff like forgetting to close the refrigerator. An entire car drive where I can't remember the journey at all. Autopilot. Conversations and words just washing over me without registering at all. The bruises and cuts I notice but when I try to recall their origins, there is a big white blank.

Then there is the anger. Seething anger. Unpredictable and inconsistent. Small stuff I feel my entire body shudder to. Almost like being premenstrual but this a more solid and smouldering red anger. At this point of my descent, in situations where I fail to get my way, I am so angry. I used to be accustomed to not getting my own way. I used to feel useless and passive and a loser when things didn't work for me. Now, hot anger. Increasing in intensity. I am feeling that lack of control that I despise and hate. Only when I'm allowing fantasies to run in my head like movies, do I feel at all in control.

ó

Denial helps me. Watching for the next wave to bulge on the horizon, I sit half submerged in a turquoise sea. I know surfing will distract me. I'm waiting. Waiting for the wave and waiting to think of nothing. To switch off. Waiting for my lower left eyelid twitch to stop. A wave is coming. I am aware of other surfers further away and they are too far to bother me. I turn my board and start to paddle at a slight angle towards the shore, ready to meet the wave. The energy is here and lifts me up so I can glide down the breaking end. Picking up speed, I tightly turn to slow up and keep within the ball of power where the wave is making white foam. After a few re-entries back into the liquid wall, I line up a last bigger turn where I try and flick over the top edge of the wave as high as I can. It folds over me, and I float across white frothy water straight towards the sand. This feels great so I head back out to sea for some more waves.

As I'm pushing the board under an incoming wave, I open my eyes and see Dave's face. I try and pretend that the whole thing isn't real and didn't actually happen. A blur is all it was, surely. I can't believe that I could or would do something so obscene and horrendous. How could I?

Another wave is upon me and I'm up and flowing along smoothly. Breaking too fast, the entire length of the wave breaks simultaneously with me in the centre heading towards shore again with white foam to my left and right. Stepping off to save myself from more paddling, I slide back on the board as the wave continues its journey without me. Surfing makes me feel so content, I can't understand why I would want to do dark stuff. Here in the sunlight out in the wide ocean, I don't make sense to myself. Thinking of the bad stuff is making me feel bad. So, why continue it? I vow that I will fill the void with good stuff. More surfing, that kind of thing. The good stuff. Pretend it was all an imagined event and never happened and won't happen. Yes, the ocean is cleansing. Cleans your body and your mind. My twitch has gone. Glinda wins.

Over the next year, I surf and surf. Glinda is in control. When small, negative occurrences happen and good things become elusive, I shift my mind into blank mode. Evillene is kept at bay. It sometimes is a serious struggle, but it is working. Eventually, I no longer see Dave's face or the blood on his bicep.

CHAPTER 11 LEXUS DRIVER

TOWARDS CHRISTMAS 2008 I COULD FEEL MY
anger and stress levels building again. The heat annoyed me,
people especially annoyed me, and the surf had been crap.
Everything buzzed in my head, and I had to do something about
it to relieve the tension. My mind-control began to
catastrophically fail.

I started to think about my huicide quest again to stage different
methods of suicide to prove how easy it is for all those Vincent
cunts to do it and get away uncaptured. I also wanted Vincent
out of my head. My first kill completely failed in deleting Vincent
from my brain. I'd wasted this bloke. Wasted his life. He should
not have gone through what I did to him. He got to me big time
and I felt bad. I felt so bad I tried not to think about any of it.
Gradually I detached further and further from him and my
emotions. I managed to not think and be blank for months. I'd
force my mind to see a white screen every time it floated back
over the bad stuff, insisting that I see all the scenes again.

I finally succumbed. My white-hot power left me. I knew it would. I was merely blocking it. It was temporary. I wanted and needed to feel. No longer could I remain blank. During the blank times, I would paddle out in big surf to try and feel something. I'd drive along way too fast zipping between cars lane changing to try and squeeze some feeling out. Once I nearly hit a truck, but I never was rewarded with adrenaline. Finally, it was stress and anger that rained down and started to fill in that void of nothing. I felt, but I felt not what I wanted to feel. Now my urge was to avoid this pain I'd managed to put on hold. The pressure increased and my compulsion to rid myself of it overtook me. To try again with a suicide staging that didn't fail formed as my solution and self-medication if you like. This time I would avoid the outdoors. I had to somehow get inside a Vincent's house.

An opportunity appeared one Sunday before Christmas. Avoca Beach has an oval near the lagoon that hosts monthly markets. I was there with Melita buying Christmas presents and eating lunch. I remember Melita and I both bought stacks of the smelly luxury goat soaps we swore we'd never buy but they make such an easy lazy present. We left around two o'clock and she was parked near the beach, but I had parked up a side street. As I walked back to the car, I walked behind a tall slim bloke, late forties and rather smartly dressed, I thought. We both pulled out onto the road and by chance, I was driving behind him. He turned off the main road into the thick of the suburb's smart houses. I realised he must live locally so I sharply turned off too and followed him. A few turns and he slowed his silver Lexus and pulled into a driveway with neatly manicured lawns and an expensive-looking double-story house. I kept driving down the road. My mind started firing up.

During the days after, when I drove to Avoca for a surf, I drove past the house hoping to see the Lexus. I saw it in the carport on the weekends but not during the week. I did one Tuesday morning 4am drive-by after work to confirm the man slept there, and it was his usual abode. The way he walked along in front of me that Sunday made me think for some reason that he had some kind of vulnerability, but I couldn't picture just what. Maybe it was just that he didn't give off an outright threatening or aggressive vibe like a lot of men do. It was more the opposite but with the all-important, generous sprinkle of arrogance. I thought I'd have a reasonable chance to overpower him physically at least. It wouldn't work for me though if he wasn't at all arrogant. My next step was to figure out how I could get him to let me into his house and what method would work as a staging. A significant thing I noted when I drove past a few times was no other car was ever there. I figured he lived alone which I felt was a bit odd for a guy like that. I never saw any kids coming or going or toys left around. He obviously had the assets to be an enticing catch for some woman. There was no gay vibe.

To get in his house I figured I'd make it easy, and walk past his house, do a little trip on the path, and hobble up to the front door and ask him for help, like a lift 'home' or borrow his phone or something. The method had to be different to the car exhaust. He wasn't that big and strong looking, but it was risky assuming that he wouldn't fight me. So, I would need to subdue him. I would use alcohol if I could.

With Dave, one main reason I staged the exhaust fumes was to mask the real way he died which was the strangling. Looking back now, I suspect I probably stuffed up there in terms of the carbon monoxide. Because he died before the fumes entered the car, he could not have inhaled them. This meant the carbon monoxide would not have shown up in any lab work or toxicology done on his body after death. The wideness and softness of the belt I used though must have worked and left no obvious imprints of the strong pressure I used flattening his windpipe. Assumptions must have been made that he had managed the gassing on purpose. With no fumes inside him but with no other information except my set-up, the officers must have been convinced enough that he had suicided. Too easy.

Too easy is my whole premise with all this.

So, if I used the same strangling technique on this next one, I'd need a new method to stage it all with. I thought the staging should also be something to do with breathing or the neck. I'm not up on the many details of what happens to bodies when they are damaged via multiple, different ways so to keep it safe for me, I try to match up the staged and the real as far as I can.

I thought about all the ways people suicide at home or in a building that are related to strangulation, and I decide on suffocation. Trying to lift a body up to stage a hanging would be too hard for me. I'm not that strong. I could either use the wide belt method and then stage with a plastic bag over the head or I could maybe just use the plastic bag. That would be safer than risking belt pressure evidence. It took me a while to work out how to get a complete stranger, someone much stronger than me, into a position that they couldn't move while I whacked a bag over their head for a few minutes. With this bloke, I didn't know if I could rely on alcohol and or medication to get him into enough of a stupor so he wouldn't thrash around like Dave did. Plan A was to try the alcohol and drugs; plan B was to tie him to something and secure him for long enough. I might need to do both.

These two plans meant I needed alcohol or medication, two ropes or equivalent and a strong plastic bag and duct tape. I needed a bag to be carrying when I 'trip' outside the house. The alcohol I thought was a problem. Who walks a long away from any shops with booze in their handbag? Around there, people drive to the local shops rather than walk. I decided to rely on him having his own supply of alcohol. He'd probably have classy stuff too. The rope I couldn't decide on, thinking it's safer to find and use something from his house and not bring anything new in but then that meant I'd have to search around, and I might not find exactly what would work. That left me just the items of drowsy drugs I could find at home, a sturdy garbage bag and tape. Thinking about the garbage bag, I nearly decided to find one from his kitchen, but I didn't want to leave anything to chance so I added that to my list with the tape. I just had to remember not to rip the duct tape with my teeth like I usually would when I handle stuff like that. I never have the patience to reach for a knife at home, but I'll take one in my bag.

I'd also leave a suicide note this time. If I'm in an individual's house, I'd have time, privacy and all his stuff to use to add to the effect of it all. That started me thinking about what to put in the note. I couldn't put in anything that I didn't know directly linked to this bloke's actual life details. If I could ask him about his life, he might divulge enough content for me. If he didn't, I could just make it like a will, spelling stuff out in terms of possessions. I predicted that someone who is wealthy might be concerned about where the material things end up and that would seem logical to an outsider. That meant I'd need to know of these things, but I could make a start and pretend he didn't finish the notes. He surely would have a computer and printer so I could use that to get around the handwriting issue.

As soon as I'd thought the whole plan out, the ruminations started. At work, in the car, at night in bed, all I could think about was doing all of it. I imagined what his muscle looked like underneath that shirt he wore. I imagined it after being sliced with a sharp blade.

CHAPTER 12 STEFAN

CHRISTMAS CAME AND WENT. STRESSFUL AS USUAL with all the crap family dynamics. New Year was a huge let down and an anticlimax. Stu seemed to spend way too much time with his mates. Then work. I really found it hard to adjust back into the factory environment during that February of 2009. The year didn't start how I was hoping. Everything annoyed me. That uncontrollable urge I truly hated, grew in me. It gnawed away at me like a parasite eating its host from the innards out. By the end of February, I had to do it to rid myself of the torment. I made up some lie to Stu one Friday and said I'd be out Saturday night. I can't remember what the excuse I gave but he didn't argue.

Ò

Saturday night, the sun was setting, and I packed my roomy, leather brown handbag with some Panadol Forte, a heavy-duty plastic bag and roll of grey duct tape, my knife and four padded nylon ropes I'd cut from one long one. The bag I was reusing from the packaging of a coffee machine that I'd bought online a month earlier. The plastic was clear and stronger than garbage bags. I also put in the bag Dave's breath freshener spray. Earlier that morning while Stu was out, I took out the ropes and made loop knots in four ends ready for me to create four quick slip knots later at speed. It took me a few goes to make the knots so there was only about a centimetre of end to spare. Handling the rope made me realise how it could cut into flesh under pressure. From the fresh laundry basket, I took four small but thick and fluffy hand towels to wrap around the ends of the rope. I undid some shoelaces from some old sneakers of Stu's, sliced them in half with scissors and wrapped that around and around the towels to fasten it onto the covered soft rope ends. I tested it around my left wrist. Only a tiny bit of the uncovered loop left a small pink mark. Later, I ditched the sneakers in the bin outside and threw some newspaper over the top.

That afternoon, I left the house in normal casual clothes and drove the twenty minutes over to Avoca. I did a fast drive-by past the man's house and yes, the Lexus was there. No other cars either. I parked in the next cross street. Then I walked back to the house. It was quite dark as I reached the front of the house. Clouds had come over and darkened everything quicker than if the sun had been out. The street was empty. I pretended to fall on the edge of the gutter and go completely down. Then I slowly limped directly for the front door. I leaned heavily against the wall and knocked on the door. I heard movement from inside. The door swung open and there was the man standing there looking down at me.

"Sorry to disturb you but I just fell over out there and hurt my foot and I'm wondering if I could just borrow your phone to try and get a lift?" I said.

"Yes of course, come in", he said looking concerned.
When he saw how much I limped along, he told me to sit down on a chair that was in the lounge room.

"Pretty dumb really, as I crossed the road, I misjudged the gutter and completely tripped over it", I said.

"Let me look at your foot."

"No, no its okay, you don't need to."

There was not much to look at of course.

"I'm actually a doctor, so I can help."

Oh no I thought. He knelt on the carpet and picked up my foot and said it was definitely not broken and had not started to swell yet.

"I think I did my back in a bit too", I said. I rubbed a patch of my upper back on the same side as the 'injured' foot.

"Do you think I could have a small drink if that's okay? I find alcohol always seems to work when my back gets sore" I said.

"Well okay, I can get you something. I've got gin and tonic is that alright?" he asked.

"That would be great, thanks."

I looked around his house while he left the room. The house was tidy and clean, not like a slobby bachelor pad. Photos of a family rested on a bookshelf. In the largest photo was him, an elegant blonde and some children posing stiffly for the camera. I could see another room which must be a study. A computer sat on the desk. He came back and as I sipped the drink, he handed me I suggested he have a drink too. I joked that I wouldn't want to be one of those types to drink alone.

"My name is Stefan by the way," he said.

"Mine's Amber. Thanks so much for the drink, it's not a good day for me, I split up with my boyfriend this morning and now this."

"Oh, that is no good."

"It'll be okay, we've not been getting along in ages so it's probably for the best I suppose. Just a bit of a shock really. Although it shouldn't be, it was on the cards."

I was rambling nervously now. I stopped and Stefan filled the space.

"Yes, I know what you mean. My wife and I haven't got along in ages."

"Where is she now?"

"Over in Hungary with the kids."

"That's not so good for you."

"No, I really miss the kids."

"Yeah, you can't just easily visit them on the weekends from here."

"No, so do you live near here Amber?" he asks changing the topic.

"Yes, a few streets away.
I wrack my brains for a street name nearby, but nothing comes to mind.

"Um up the hill."

"Do you think that marriage counselling stuff helps people?" I asked quietly. I was thinking a while back some relationship counselling might work for me and my boyfriend.

"Nah, I don't know if counselling helps with anything. Talking through stuff, how does that even do anything?"

"Yeah, I agree. Maybe drugs to numb the pain?" I ventured.

"No, I don't bother with drugs. Just must try and get through it really. We all just have to get on with it don't you think?"
He said this last bit in a patronising tone, and it felt like he believed he was somehow better than me. He didn't need any help because he was too good for it. This annoyed me. It's the arrogance I had detected in him before. I could see it in the way he held himself. Even though it annoyed me, this attitude is what I needed to fire me up. Nice guys just don't do it for me.

"Who was it you are going to call?" He then asked in an irritated way.

"Oh, it was my boyfriend, umm ex-boyfriend. I forgot. I can't really ring him. I'll be alright, my place is not far. I should be able to walk there, soon."
I rubbed my back, and to reach it, I lifted my top up a bit, slightly suggestively. Out of the corner of my eye, I could see Stefan glance at my chest. Wincing, I struggled to place my hand on the 'sore' spot.

"Do you want another gin?"

"Yes please, thanks, Stefan. That will help, I'm sure."
He came back with two more refills. One for him and one for me.

Can you see anything? I asked while I leaned over forward

and lifted my shirt up more and off my skin. Stefan put his crystal tumbler down and walked around behind me.

"You can pull my shirt up more if you like, I don't mind." He did this and I tried to explain where it hurt.

"Do you mind rubbing it just a bit? He placed his palm on my skin and slowly pushed into my skin while rubbing over it."

"That's actually really very good Stefan. I rewarded him like a master with their dog."

He widened the area of massaging to take in both sides of my back. Taking that as a cue, I pulled my top over my head and dropped down on the floor. Stefan stopped rubbing and pressing and I thought maybe I'd misjudged him and pushed him too far, but he had just stopped to take a rather large swig of his gin. Resuming the massage, we were both silent. It seemed like a long time we were in this position. Then, Stefan broke the spell and started talking about how bad the recent fires in Victoria were. I sensed he felt uncomfortable.

"Yeah, I think the news said 179 people died. Not good when they are all so innocent and so underserving of death," I said.

I had to get him back on track. Back to positive things.

"Maybe it's time to repay you," I said.

A weird splutter came from his mouth, but I couldn't see his face to try and read his expression.

"Just a return favour for the back rub you gave me, is all I meant."

He didn't seem too enthused about sex with a stranger, but my aim was to get him somewhere else where I could somehow get the ropes on him.

"And maybe this is how we both, um, move on. When was the last time you've had a back rub anyway? Ages I bet."

"Yeah, I guess."

"If I could just use your bathroom, then I'll give you a back rub, but it'll have to be on a bed or something because of my injuries."

"All right."

I leave my shirt off and put on an awkward rise from the chair.

I collect my handbag from the floor and start for the hallway.

"It's first on the right down there."

I can feel his eyes on my exposed black lacy bra.

ó

Before using the toilet, I reached deep into my handbag, pulled out the ropes and formed the slip knots, placing them back carefully so they are on top and easy to reach. Trying not to make any noise, I carefully look in his bathroom cabinet. Not much in the way of medications, only some Somac for heartburn. I thought there might be something useful for later, for maybe another one down the track. This should be the last one though, this should sort me out for good. This should erase Dave's face and Vincent's forever. NO more down the track!

We walk slowly upstairs to a bedroom that I assume is the main one. Stefan had a different glass in his hand and handed me one.

"Just water. I expect you want one too."

Again, I detected some slight irritation from him.

"My wife always complains I'm selfish so here you go, have this."

He thrust the glass into my hand.

I drank it down and smiled seductively at him.

"Your turn now."

I pointed at the bed noticing it had no obvious tie up points on the bedhead or the end of the bed. I didn't think Stefan would go for being tied up for sex so another tactic would have to be tried.

"This man once told me there is a good thing about becoming blind and that is how he can totally focus on the sense of touch. He said that everyone should do things blindfolded now and then to get more out of the touching sensations." I paused.

"And this friend of mine also reckons the parts of the body that are used a lot need to be massaged to reenergise them. Not just the back but the hands and feet and arms. There is supposed to be pressure points in the wrists and ankles."

"Yeah right," Stefan said a bit sarcastically.

"Well anyway, I am going to give you all of this and then you tell me whether you still think it's a crock, okay?"

"Oh, I guess, if you have to."

He takes his shirt off and it's thin and folds nicely into a blind fold that I tie as tight as I can round the back of his head. He argues that he is going to be lying on his stomach and doesn't need the blindfold, but I explain that to be comfortable, he needs to have his head to the side and that's where he can get light come in that will spoil it. While he is lying there, I pull out Dave's breath spray and spray his neck lightly. Next, I silently pull out the first rope and put in on the bed near his right hand and start massaging his hands.

"Like eating dinner with silver cutlery, where you start from the outside and eat to the inside with the dessert spoon left for last, I am going to massage your outside bits, hands and feet and then work my way in to the centre."

Picking up his right hand and arm, I press my fingers into his flesh and gently put the rope circle over and around his wrist. I keep massaging and then put his arm down but forward and stretched out in front.

"You can't move at all, or it won't work."

As I move to the left hand, after encircling it with the rope, I reach down and loop the end of the rope around the corner leg of the bed and tighten the knot but without tension. I quietly repeat this on his other side. He is now restrained but doesn't know it. I smoothly start on the left hand pressing and pushing and stroking, all the time warning him not to move a muscle. At one point he complains he has an itchy calf muscle, so I reach back and scratch it for him. Slowly with one hand pushing into his last ankle, I ever so quietly pull up the bag and then the duct tape, but I can't find the knife with my one hand feeling around searching. I know it's there though. Then I climb swiftly up and straddle Stefan's back. I reach forward and lift the side of his head up with my left hand and push the open end of the plastic bag back towards me while pulling down the blindfold. Stefan thrusts his head back with a yelp while simultaneously straining against the rope. This helps me slide the bag to its end like a condom to completely have his head inside. I must lean down to get the tape and then I use all my weight on his back to hold him down. Pulling hard on the tape, I get enough out to start wrapping around the neck to seal his head fully inside the plastic bag with it's finite volume of air. I just wrap around and around while Stefan's head bobs up and down. Moisture gathers inside and the clearness goes out of it. The tape somehow sticks to itself, so I just leave the lot as it is. There is plenty there and it's keeping the whole thing in place. His raspy gasping noises filled the room.

Later, when I analysed what I'd done for mistakes, I realised it was lucky I couldn't find the knife in the end because there is no way a suiciding suffocating person would be able to or even bother to cut off the end of the tape anyway. If I had followed through with that, someone may have noticed and become suspicious that perhaps no suicide happened at all but rather a homicide befell Stefan.

By the time I had the bag secured, Stefan's attempts at thrashing started to slow. That meant it was safe for me to get off him and look at what was happening to him. I knelt next to his head and could see some of his face. His body still moving and the bag completely sucking the plastic across his face and into his mouth, then out again. One last big suck in, and his eyes changed. It seemed the exact moment of transition to death took slightly longer than with Dave. Stefan seemed alive from his eyes even though his body no longer moved. A moment passed and then the eyes changed again to dead and dull. Whooshing out he went to wherever. Here he is alive and then here he is just not. He is not in the room anymore because there is no life in the room or in the body. How can the life bit leave? The living bit is so strong and then it's suddenly, absolutely, and completely gone. I felt intrigued but also confused. I felt energised and somehow it was also a let-down. I wished I could make him alive again. I stared at his naked arms. Then I pulled out my penknife from my handbag and cut into a bicep just a bit. Some blood settled on the surface. I wiped the blade on the edge of one of the hand towel bindings.

6

Now I had to finish the rest of my plan. After undoing the knots and taking off all the ropes, I turned the body over. It nearly slid off the side of the bed and onto the floor at one point. The bag remained intact with the tape. The arms I positioned next to the body, the right arm a bit further out and the legs a slightly apart. The wrists and ankles did not seem to show significant marks. The ropes and hand towels now back in my handbag, I left the room and headed for the office.

Stefan had not told me anything about possessions he had and there was no way to guess specific items that I could put into a suicide note. I forgot to ask him. Thinking his computer might hold clues that I could use, I switched it on. Scanning his files didn't really help. What was worse was I tried to get the printer to work, and it just wouldn't. That was how I'd planned to write the suicide note, by typing it on his own computer. Opening his internet browser, I typed in keywords of suicide and helium. A few websites came up that were help sites. I typed in a few other ways of suiciding and then left the computer on.

Rummaging around in his office, I discovered some handwritten documents. I took some lined paper he had and wrote a suicide note by copying his handwriting. The loops on the letters and the strokes he used were distinctive to him and easy to copy. The contents of the letter stumped me for a while. I can't remember now exactly what I wrote. I had to wander through the house to pick up some details to include. His family's names were not on the back of the photos I saw in the lounge room, but I did find them in different rooms of the house. These names I included and wrote a note to the wife and separate notes to the children saying how sorry 'I am' and how 'I love you' and to 'forgive me', that kind of thing. Things became a bit of blur for a while there. I think I placed them on the kitchen table, but I don't remember doing that. All I remember is the dead eyes. Next thing I'm walking up a hill back to my car. As soon as I unlocked the car and sat down in the driver's seat, I checked my brown handbag for everything. Relieved, I found the ropes, towels, shoelaces, the knife and an extra item, the Lexus keychain. I vaguely remember unclipping the keys that dangled from it and throwing it into the handbag. This I took because I had spent time during my drive-bys, fixated on whether the Lexus was in the drive or not. This represented him.

It wasn't till I'd driven back towards home and over the Rip Bridge that the enormity of what I'd just done started soaking into my consciousness. This felt like flipping over from one person to another and is not pleasant. Instead of going home, I drove aimlessly until I found myself at a park at Woy Woy at one of the main boat ramps. Grateful no one was around at this end of the park, I backed the car in and turned the engine off. This massive mess of conflict swept over me. On one hand I had achieved what I set out to do and provided another example to the world that people like Vincent are out there getting away with murder by staging suicides. On the other, I felt guilt at what I had done. I tried to tell myself ridiculous things to try and relieve the anxiety of taking someone's life. Of taking someone's life, again. Repulsion of what I did. This bloke wasn't even that arrogant and didn't really resemble Vincent much at all. Why did I do it? At that moment, a grizzled old man with a white beard stared blankly at me as he shuffled past. I stared back at him.

My denial tactics finally kicked in, so power and strength took over. You did it because there are too many arrogant men out there. Take one of these fucks out of the system and lots of people gain. Especially his kids. Later, that's what really wrecked my head. The photos of his children sent guilt waves through me and then my fucked-up brain managed to twist that to thinking they would be better off thanks to me! This conflicting yo yo like effect of what I was doing became incredibly tiring and started to make me more and more angry with everything and everyone. This meant I became desperate to do whatever I could to take the anger away.

During the days and weeks after Stefan, I became depressed. I couldn't understand why the exhilaration of killing didn't last. All that work and I'm feeling worse than before. My project worked and I'm still not satisfied. I just didn't get why. At least there was nothing in the papers about Stefan so that crucial part of it succeeded. No jail. Triumph over the authorities never came into it for me as one might imagine it would—my aim was to help society by doing these killing, so I was not putting my middle finger up at all. Authorities have a job to do, and I was just trying to help them see a few gaps. Today I understand that there are more effective ways of helping society than taking people out, but back then my mind became locked up tight in a steel box and I didn't know how to break out of my own imprisonment of horrifically flawed ideals and fantasies. I'd managed to remove Dave's face but now Stefan's face and eyes haunted me at random, inopportune times.

CHAPTER 13 SKILLION

MY RAGE RAMPED UP UNTIL I HAD TO DO
something to make it go away. Angry at work, angry at home
and angry in the surf. Monotonous and disempowering. I knew
that doing something to relieve the stress would take the edge
off for me. A new plan was the answer. A third method of
suicide and maybe something outdoors this time. The cliff jump
would be a good one. A push over the edge for the actual
homicide and a suicidal leap as the stage. Living by the ocean
there are plenty of hefty cliffs up and down the coast. Some
secluded and some not so.

One grey, wet and rainy day, when a fierce southerly wind
had been whipping up the seas for a few days, I drove to Terrigal
to The Skillion to glean some ideas. Like The Gap at Watson's
Bay, this is a magnet for suicidal people. Parking the car just left
of the grassed rampart, I looked out the windscreen to the rough
seas in front. I clicked on the windscreen wiper to scrape off the
salty and fresh waters thrown up onto it. The water was right
there, wild, and just metres from the car. An old dark blue
Holden sedan pulled up right next to me and this loser in the
driver's seat started looking over at me. Then he's leaning

forward and cocking his ugly head towards me, grinning like a complete fuck up. No other people were around due to the bad weather. Did this fuck want a fuck or was he doing code for a drug deal? I'm not up on that stuff. I tried to ignore him, and I locked all four doors when he wasn't looking. I couldn't see the cliffs from the rain pelting sideways, but I could see the turbulent waves thrashing about outside.

I looked at the idiot next to me and imagined my fingertips on his neck feeling his heartbeat stop as his eyes change to dead. I could hardly see his face with the rain, but I wonder if the whites of his eyes will look so googly and round, compared to when in the throes of death. I can also see myself dragging him down the rocky boulders in front and into the sea. A monstrous wave would come up, cover him over and suck him back out to its submerged black lair, way out to sea. Never to be seen again. He must have read my mind because he backed out of there and drove away. It was my turn to grin.

My raincoat covered most of me as I puffed up the hill to the top of the Skillion. Two fences surrounded the sheer cliff at the top with a newer painted steel fence at the lookout part and an old rusted worn out fence closer to the cliff edge. This second fence held tenuously onto the high cliff edge and seemed so low to the ground you could step over it and be gone. Hardly a deterrent. Looking to the north I could see the cliff over there to be scarily high too but without the fences. I couldn't see much to the south in the conditions. On the way down a brass plaque told of someone's death. Many deaths have happened here and many more will. There is no respect for suicidal people at the Skillion. The old rusty end-of-the-line fence is the last uncaring insult. It represents the attitude of a council who couldn't give a crap about the community. If, say, Debbie had decided she couldn't take any more abuse from Vincent and went up there to jump but couldn't quite decide, she'd see the broken-down scrappy fence and take it personally. She would think,

"That's meant to be easy to get over because no one in the world cares about me and it's not strong or tall enough to stop me so I'm going to do it, right now."

And over she'd go. Complete shit. If they mow the lawn to make it pretty for aesthetics, can't they spend the same energy and a bit of money and fix up the fencing to save those people who are suicidal and need other peoples' help? Bastards.

Vincent crashing through that fence would be good though. With that thought I run down the hill back to the car. I slip halfway down and sprawl onto my shoulder. I'm okay, just more soaked. I can't be bothered to walk around the other cliffs as I planned. Too cold and too wet plus I don't want googly eyes to come back while I'm out of the car. These are the times that I wish I was either a bloke or a big burly type of woman. Then I could intimidate people before they tried anything on me, and I wouldn't have to feel threatened by anyone. Men take it for granted that they can get around pretty much unhindered. Sexual undertones and overtones tend to seep into so many interactions I have with men which is fine mostly, except for not knowing when some fruity-tune fuck can overpower me. Sometimes I wear baggy tops that hide my big breasts to minimise that kind of attention. Around this time though, I remember feeling extra confidence and inner strength thanks to my interactions with Postie and Lexus man. During the drive home I think about the staging part that goes with a cliff jump. The huicide. One thing I read about is that people who jump or who walk into the sea to end their lives often take off pieces of their clothing before they go. These items are shoes which they will position neatly near the edge, sometimes watches or jewellery. Any clothing they will carefully fold up and leave close by. This denotes a suicide to be different from an accident or a homicide. Opened and consumed alcohol bottles or blister packs of medication at the top would not be out of place either. No need for a note then.

Homicide method and suicide staging type combined with a location ticked off, I am nearly ready with my next huicide. Now all I needed to do is work out how to get someone to the location and then near the edge but also find a suitable Vincent to punish.

CHAPTER 14 THEFTS

ONE NIGHT AT THE FACTORY, MELITA, ROCKY
and I were on Line 7 packing small quiches into boxes. Melita
and Rocky talked about stealing. Rocky was saying how he nicks
stuff occasionally from the shops and Melita seemed shocked. I
just listened and pretended to be in my conveyor monotony
stupor. You just do the motions and zone out to everything. No
drugs necessary. Melita started quizzing Rocky.

"So, what kind of things do you steal?"

"Oh, you know, maybe a shirt from K-Mart or some
chocolate at Coles."

"Have you ever been caught?"

"Yeah once, years ago."

"What happened?"

"I was in year 7 at high school and we were holidaying at
some caravan park up the coast at Port Stephens. All I did was
tax some gay baseball hat from the general stall up there. I kind
of put it on my head with the tags tucked under and walked out.
I crossed the road and thought I was home and hosed when this
burly security guard, all trussed up in his uniform, came up
behind me and put his hand on my shoulder."

"You didn't run?"

"I thought about it but, I hate to admit it, back then I was too scared of this guy. He was huge. I suppose the uniform was intimidating too. Anyway, he asked me about the hat and told me to take it off. I handed it over, tags still attached. He called the cops and I had to give a statement and have my dad come in who was absolutely spewing at me."

"Did you get a conviction or anything?"

"Nah, they let me off with a warning and the shop owner banned me from going in his shop again. Fair enough I suppose."

"What made you do it?"

"Me mates at school had this idea of each of us steal something and bring it to school after the holidays. The riskier the better. We had been talking about how boring holidays can be so we thought this would spice it up a bit. The annoying thing was, when I saw them after the holidays, they all had excuses as to why they hadn't stolen anything. I was the only dipshit that did it and got caught."

"But you still steal now?"

"Yeah, but only now and then and nothing major. They say that the prices are bumped up in the big chain shops to kind of counter the losses from theft anyway."

I'm listening to this conversation and am just glad they don't involve me, or I'd have to lie to them. Something I don't enjoy. They would be completely shocked if I enlightened them about my stealing expertise. It's simply something I do naturally. Sounds bad I know but it's just the way it is for me. Initially I decided to steal something in an attempt to be rewarded by an adrenaline rush. It wasn't that I wanted the item, I wanted the rush. Maybe the first few things gave me that and then I felt nothing. Ripped off is what I felt.

6

Now, I take precautions to try and curb my habit of taking things. It's a bit of a bad habit and it's so easy to do but I don't want to be caught and it's not a good thing to be doing. One shop I felt guilty stealing from was the baggage shop in a plaza. I should say one lady I stole from rather than one shop I stole from. It was the lone struggling lady that I took the big brown leather handbag from, not a shop. Later, I got the guilts, every time I walked past and saw her. I felt sorry for her because there was never anyone much in there buying her products and she probably was on her way to going bust. From then on, I restricted myself to larger businesses. The easiest one which I am sure lots of people take advantage of is the self-serve checkouts of Woolworths and Coles supermarkets. That is where it's too risky for me to use the self-serve because my self-control is not always there and I'm likely to steal.

Minute details I've picked up when cruising a large shopping complex is to avoid wearing black or aggressive looking clothes. Shop guards will hover around you like blow flies, waiting to land on you. Items you can wear are always good to nick. I especially like the psychological kick of pilfering an item from the counter right in front of the shop keeper.

Charity shops I will pay money for although I get annoyed at some of the old bats for not rounding down and giving me a better price than what's marked. More and more of them count the whole lot diligently instead of saying,

"I'll give that to you for just x amount, love. That's fine."

Sometimes I'll steal from individuals with no qualms. Not my friends or family except occasionally the relatives that I don't respect. If I happen to find cash on the street there is no way I will ask around if anyone has lost it. Those idiots would just say,

"Yeah, I just dropped that, that's mine, give it back."

My windfall then becomes theirs instead. My stealing habits are not usually planned, more opportunistic. If something comes up and I want it, then usually I take it. One time there was a man in the street with a flash red mountain bike. I saw him wheel his bike next to a car near some houses. He then went inside a house. As I walked past, I just jumped on the bike and took off like a bat out of hell. Out of sight and out of earshot within thirty seconds I was. I rode it along a track and stashed it off the side so no one could see it. This was a bit tricky due to its bright colouring. Being a sunny day also meant it gleamed. A big spreading bush solved that problem. This bike was not something I could just continue to ride through the streets. After hiding it, I later returned with my car and a bike helmet. I walked along the track, pulled out the bike as quick as I could, put the helmet on and rode it along the track to the car, crammed it into the boot and drove away. Easy peasy. No commotion from the man because he didn't have a clue who took it or which direction it went. No one much around either, only a courier saw me when I struggled cramming the bike into the boot. When Stu asked me where the bike came from, I told him one of my friends from work sold it to me for a hundred bucks. I suggested he should buy one too so we could go riding together. I backed the story further by saying how I had had the bike helmet for ages with the aim to go buy a bike and now I finally did. The bike helmet was one I'd found during a council pickup day when people threw out their bulk trash and left it on the side of the road next to their house. I always thought it would come in handy and it did. If anyone had asked the courier about a bike thief, he would have discounted me due to the helmet I wore. What thief would bother to wear a helmet and if a thief just took someone's bike from outside someone's house opportunistically, they wouldn't be prepared with a helmet as cover, surely? In his mind he had already dismissed me as a typical bike rider and forgotten me. The out of place details are what people remember more, I reckon.

One entertaining theft was from David Jones. A friend of mine and Debbie's was engaged. I stole an expensive and elegant silver Tiara from the accessory section and gave it to Julie-Ann. Just for a joke, I recited to her my version of the bridal rhyme for her.

"Something old, something new, something stolen, something blue."
Her expression of shock was so amusing."

"No not really, I meant to say something borrowed not something stolen. I hope you like it."

"Oh of course I love it! You always buy such cool gifts!" Yeah, I wonder how, I thought, given my crap income back then as a veterinary nurse. People are so dumb. Stu had no clue either. One time I managed to find a new diving watch still in its packaging at a Jumble sale. He assumed I paid top dollar for it.

These are always easy pickings. It's only one or two individuals that you must position yourself around to block their view while items either go up your sleeve, into a bag, pocket, under a jumper or just put on and worn. Why no guilts for them, but lots for the bag lady, I can't say. All I can think of is the more I did it the more I didn't think about it. People have preconceived ideas about what thieves look like and their behaviour. This is the same for killers. People assume a young girl who is polite and seems normal, could not and would not do away with another person.

Its people who are the suckers. Living in their dumb closed worlds, slaves to societal pressures and rules. It is so freeing to not live like that. To reach the ultimate heights of non-conformity, I suspect takes time. It is the steps I took over years in that direction that led me to do what I did. It is a steady progression from say, skipping school and nicking lollies, to speeding in cars and stealing jewellery to then say break and enter and residential theft. From personal theft to killing is not a super big stretch. It is just a matter of switching off from the other end of it. It's best to have no empathy with the other person involved but sometimes some passion, rage and anger is necessary to go through with the whole thing and finish it.

On occasion, I have broken into a few houses. This wasn't so much to steal stuff but just more out of curiosity and for the vibe of it. These houses were not around where I live, but further north at Forster during holidays. Holiday houses are easy in that it is usually obvious when they are occupied and when they are not. Clothes on the line, bins in or out on the street. Bins still out days after pickup is a sure clue that no one is home and importantly, no neighbours look out for the owners of that particular house. Spare keys are surprisingly easy to find around the house, under the mat even. If no keys, then often I can usually find a loose window that can be pushed open. Inside, there's often some cash somewhere and alcohol. Occasionally a pretty ornament will catch my eye too. I never make a mess nor take everything of the one type of item. I'll take the partially drunk bottle of spirits and leave the unopened one. That way whoever it is will just think they must have drunk it last time.

Once or twice, on a stinking hot night, I skinny dipped in their pools. At one stylish house, well stocked with bottles of wine, I swam around in their narrow lap pool while intermittently drinking an entire bottle of their champagne. Stu never knew. Either we had an argument, and I'd stormed out the door or I couldn't sleep after his snoring took hold. Partial moon nights worked the best. Just enough light to see everything and not too much that I couldn't blend into the night in my black attire. This sort of double life I enjoy. I just didn't realise where it would lead me. If I had known, then I would have done all I could to prevent myself from walking the horrendous dark path that I did. It's the little barriers of the brain that are broken down one by one and you are finally left with a life with zero boundaries. No demarcation anymore to tell you when to stop venturing further outwards.

Without the set bold font bordered patterns of living a life like most people, life can become more difficult in some ways. It becomes easier to succumb to urges and impulses. To resist is hard. This is reinforced every time I succeeded in some kind of action without raising suspicion or getting caught. My ego swelled and I felt invincible especially immediately after whatever it was, I was doing. This euphoria wanes and I want another hit. So off I go and do whatever it was again. The smaller scale activities I did would get boring and I think that might be one reason why I up scaled to worse stuff. To get the same conquering feeling, I had to try something new and different. The reason I'm explaining this all now is that I don't want to keep on this nightmare rollercoaster of trying to feed my ravenous ego, or self, or whatever you want to name it. In fact, I can't keep it up. The good thing is now, as I write, I'm looking back at me from like an out-of-body experience. I am looking down at my psychological thoughts from afar, from the ceiling like I am a dead person myself but also live, sitting in a chair. Seeing the gaps of my thoughts and joining up the holes I realise how weak and stupid I have been, but not now in the present. I am awake now. Awake to me and my past. I am struggling to believe I acted like I have and did all those terrible things to people. But denial no longer is an option. To repent if you like, I must accept responsibility that yes that was me, I did do this stuff. It was me and not someone else. I let myself get to this point. No one else. I finally have an insight into why some murderers take their own lives. A glimpse of their blackness and their weakness is so overwhelming. They fail to deal with it. They fail to transform themselves into someone strong. Someone strong enough to resist themselves. They give up. They give up. I won't give up trying to change myself for the better.

6

I say I won't give up but the building of pressure after a huicide seemed to come on faster each time. After Stefan it didn't take long at all. I felt like I must figure out my next move or the gnawing will consume me. So, Friday nights, Stuart drinks at the pub with the boys. What works here is the window of time I can exploit while Stu is out. As a protective measure, I should choose a whole different scenario than that first time, to limit any patterns I may make and leave behind. I know creating patterns in human behaviours can be very hard to avoid. Maintaining habits and selecting the familiar is our natural tendency, just like choosing the same seat on the train every time or filling up at the same petrol station. But I must resist these temptations.

It's like I'm stuck in a circular feeding hell where the more my thoughts are of doing deletions, the more intense everyone and everything is, and I struggle more to keep the pressure down. The more I do the more I have to do. A large part of me knows I desperately need some form of circuit breaker and just stop, but I'm in it too deep to find one and claw my way out. I do try though, for whatever that's worth.

CHAPTER 15 ROCKY

A MONTH LATER, AT THE FACTORY, I THINK IT WAS an early, maybe four am start, Melita and I are on Bites in the cool room with Rocky. We all wore our daggy tracksuits, to keep warm. Rocky is a twenty something, laid back kind of guy who is always positive and energetic. Time travels quickly when the three of us are together and we are positioned on the conveyor close enough to talk. Bites is a satisfying one for my sweet tooth too. Small rectangles of vanilla ice cream are coated in chocolate, and they are carried along the conveyor belt, often stuck together. We slide the joined ones off and fill small cardboard boxes with the rest. A few we deftly pop in our mouths. It doesn't take long before I'm feeling queasy. Rocky is telling us as usual about last Saturday night at the pub at Toukley and how he loves how there is always something happening there. Brawls, drunk women, and men going right off with people hauled out by the bouncers. This time, Rocky described how it was a burly bouncer who was king-hit in the head and collapsed. He lay on the carpet, completely out to it, until paramedics took him off to hospital, siren blaring. Rocky didn't see who clobbered him, as he and his mates always sit off to the side and avoid the melees. He also mentioned the platinum blonde girls, always hanging around at closing time waiting to be picked up. Then he said with a sneer,

"And there's always some ugly geezer leaving with them."

"Eeewwwww!" Melita and I both said simultaneously said as we both looked down the line to Joseph, a most unattractive forty something wannabe sleazebag who is always chatting up the newbies, especially if they are blonde.

When this particular gross guy gets too close and talks to you, he reveals oversized oblongs of yellow upper teeth and contaminates the space with his filthy, sewer breath. Melita told me once when she first smelt him, she mistook his breath for a fart. That cracked me up. We referred to Joseph from then on as FB as in Fart Breath.

What Rocky said about ugly geezers started me thinking. I'm not one to know the etiquette of picking up men at a bar but I'm wondering if it might be a good choice of location to find myself a loser. A loser minus the farty breath. Debbie's face appears before me and is then gone just as quick. The questions I then ask Rocky, I hope will answer this. Certain things I need to know about someone if I'm to manage another successful huicide. I'm not sure if I can find things out in that environment though. Well, more to the point, I'm not sure if I can pull it off, being a girl ready to pick up and go home with some complete stranger. What happens when you reject people in a pub, or you can't get rid of them? This might sound incongruous to what I did with Dave but imagining entering a bar on your own and hanging there and then socialising with drunk egotistical men with the end point of sex is rather unsettling to me. I think I'd feel too vulnerable, and I'd rather be in control of the situation. If I had an excuse to be there that's not to specifically meet someone, then that would be easier. I can pick and choose more easily because they won't assume I'm there solely to meet someone. Therefore, they won't be so annoyed if I reject them. Poker machines might just do this for me. I asked Rocky if there's pokies there and he said nope. The more I mulled this idea over, the more I started to obsess a bit. I had to find a pub or club with pokies, well away from home. The last thing I wanted was someone I knew to see me picking up men. Maybe I should even get a wig just in case. That would help for cameras too I suppose. Especially if things fail to run to plan. Something I know is a reality, no matter how meticulous I am.

CHAPTER 16 PLANNING

I SETTLED ON A CLUB UP NEAR LONG JETTY IN
the next shire of Wyong about fifty minutes away driving north.
The idea is I'd drive up there on the next Friday afternoon that
Stu was at drinks and see what I could find myself. This also had
to be when I didn't have a shift at work. The factory operated
twenty-four hours a day but not weekends. My work was on call,
and I worked on a casual basis usually at night. Even though
work stopped over the weekend, I could still be called in
Thursday night or Friday morning early although four shifts in
a week was the maximum I'd be allowed to do for safety reasons.
This means that by the end of the week, I'd know if there was a
possibility or not of a call in.

A few weeks before Easter before I thought I'd go to the club;
I was surfing at North Avoca as the sand banks there were good,
and the change of my usual surf break refreshed me. As I walked
out of the sea another surfer who had been surfing into the same

rip catching lefts while I had been catching right handers, finished too. We headed for the same walkway off the sand. I think he'd been looking at me a bit when we were out in the water. Our paths merged and we started talking about the waves and stuff. I said I needed a breather and sat down on the beach thinking he would say bye and keep going but he didn't. He stopped and stood next to me looking down. Then he started chatting me up.

"Not working today?"

"Nah worked yesterday and again tonight."

This is not an unusual question for surfers when you are surfing mid-week. People like to gauge whether you are on the dole or have a job.

"What about you?"

He sat down and explained how he just lost his job and that he was making the most of it. The water was not too cold yet to be wearing a wetsuit and he only wore board shorts. This guy seemed late twenties and slightly stocky like he'd played footy. Mild beer gut protruding. Then he kind of just got this look and stared shamelessly at my bust. My mind processed two things, his words of assumption that I'm a bludger and his leery act. I realised I could bring him down a notch or more. Many more in fact.

We talked and I asked him if he had a girlfriend and he said he'd just split up from one, and she turned out to be a bitch. I'm thinking double bonus here.

"We'll have to meet up for drinks somewhere sometime."

"For sure."

"Easter's coming up, how about then?"

"Yeah."

We eventually decided on Sunday night because we both had stuff on the other days. I'd make up some innocent reason to tell Stu that I'm out Sunday night. Even though I didn't know how I'd work it in, I suggested a pub further north, but he preferred the local one. It felt like there was an urgency to run with this or lose the opportunity completely. We'd confirm the venue later and swap numbers at the cars. We talked some more, and he told me he worked in a coal mine in the Hunter but came originally from Lithgow. His dad, him and his brother all worked in the collieries around Lithgow but when his old man retired a few years ago, the whole family moved to the Central Coast. He lives by himself at Avoca. He used to play footy in Lithgow with his brother Matt but hasn't kept it up since living on the coast. Instead, he took up surfing again. He learnt as a kid when the family sometimes visited relatives up at San Remo during the summer holidays. His name is Byron.

Brushing the gritty sand from our bums, Byron walked away a few feet and picked up his towel and car keys and we walked together to the car park. I stood near his late model, white commodore wagon, putting my board down on the ground while he unlocked it.

"Give us your phone and I'll put my number in it."

He handed it to me and as I looked at it, I said I had to just go and get my phone for a second as I couldn't remember my new number. I walked away, took my key from my wetsuit, unlocked my car, and then quickly searched through Byron's contacts. I found a Matt and phew there was only one. This I assume is his brother Matt. I started a text and included Matt and a few other blokey type names I could find in his contacts.

"Just lost me job and me girlfriend. Life's complete shit right now but I'll be ok as usual".

I sent it off, located his number next and wrote it on a note pad I store in the glove box. Then I wasted a bit of time pulling my wetsuit off, slipping on some shorts over my bikini, combing my hair. Then I scrolled back to the text I'd sent and deleted it from his phone. No way did I want him seeing that. The message though was now out there, and I'd seeded the vibe to Byron's family and friends that not all was good for Byron right now and things could possibly be heading further south for him soon. I pass his phone back through the window as he sat in the driver's seat of his white commodore and fibbed to him how I can't find my phone and that I must have left it at home. Then I waited a half second to see if he reacted, thinking I was backing out and his face did seem to change and stiffen. At least I think it did.

I'm not the best at reading faces unfortunately. I laughed and assured him that I wrote his number down and I'd call him next week. Relief I then saw.

"Awesome see ya then."

He swivelled his head towards me out the window with his leery kind of lopsided grin, as he backed his car, swung the wheel then one last look at my cleavage and away he went. Yeah 'awesome' I thought. You won't be thinking that for too much longer surfer boy.

CHAPTER 17 SURFER BOY

I'D STARTED TO FEEL ALIVE AGAIN. THE
mundaneness of my life is about to be put aside for a while. We
could meet in the car park at Byron's choice of the Terrigal Pub.
I'd have to do wear a hat and maybe some glasses to not be easily
recognisable by anyone that knows me, such as other workers
from the factory. We'd have drinks. Me, Lemon Lime and
Bitters, him lots of anything as long it's stronger than beer. Then
we'll drive somewhere else with the lure of something sexual and
more drinks I'd bought along. We'd drive in his car to some
secluded location. Not sure where yet but I'm starting to think
the Skillion is convenient on a few levels. People are known to
suicide off the large ramp into the sky. As I explained it's a bit
like The Gap at Watson's Bay in Sydney's eastern suburbs. The
Gap sucks people to it from all over Sydney to end their lives
there. Like The Gap, The Skillion draws people for the Central
Coast. The cliff jump near The Skillion is what I decided for
Surfer Boy's impending huicide. There he could drink, get
excessively drunk and yeah 'jump' to his death because of his
terribly depressed state. Then I'd walk back to my car that I'd
parked somewhere between the Terrigal Pub and Terrigal beach.

I'd walk along the beach and be dressed in a way I could look gender neutral and dark so I would not be noticed. Like black slacks and I'd take an oversized black jumper with a hoody. To meet up with him, I'd take in a black bag everything I needed such as clothes and drinks. Things, however, didn't go to plan.

Ⓞ

To not leave any electronic thread of me connecting to Byron I continued to keep my phone out of the equation. This meant ringing him from a supposedly untraceable phone. That week after first meeting Byron, as I drove around the place going to work, the shops and the usual, I had a frustrating time trying to locate a quiet public phone booth. It had to be in a quiet place so I could hear. I tried one on the main road I take to work over at Lisarow, but trucks and traffic completely obliterated any sounds coming out of the receiver, so I hung up. I found one down at Killcare Beach when I did a surf check there one afternoon. He didn't answer and it swallowed my coins without me even saying a word. The side of my foot ached all that afternoon after I kicked the wall of the booth. I nearly went back the next day but luckily, I spied another one closer to home and stopped when the traffic had eased and wasn't bustling and noisy.

Byron sounded upbeat when I got through. I suggested we meet at the Terrigal Pub on the Sunday night and share a few bevvies together, just him and me like. I needed to make sure he takes his car there so I hinted he should bring his commodore as it's such a spacious wagon if 'you know what I mean'. It would be a disaster if he was dropped off at the pub by a friend or something. 'Sweet', Byron agreed. Byron now sorted out, I told Stu how I'd been invited to go over to Melita's place to have dinner that night and it was a bit of a girl's thing with her mum and her kids, and he'd be bored if he went too. I thought Stu would be happy with this, but he seemed a bit pissed at me. All I had to do next was organise the bits and pieces I might need for this next deletion.

Ó

Speedy. My life seemed to have shifted up a gear. Everything seemed to go a little faster. I also felt more volatile. Explosive but weirdly contained. I found it increasingly hard to pull back and be everyday with everyone, when in my head I relentlessly, ferociously despised them all.

At the bottle shop I chose bourbon again but not cans. Two bottles of Cougar. I'm not going to spoil him with Jack Daniels. I figured Byron is a bourbon type. Another reason I chose bourbon is it is one spirit I can handle better than scotch, rum, or vodka. The worst type for me must be the one you drink with the lime and salt and the worm. Tequila, I think it is. I'll show him a display of sharing drinks together to keep up the mood, but that will be it. Potent spirits will be faster acting than beer or wine too, plus the mixed cola should mask the codeine flavour I'll add. At the supermarket I buy a 750 ml bottle of caffeine and sugar free Pepsi drink. Caffeine and sugar I'm thinking are uppers when I really want to thump home downers in double quick time.

Ó

Sunday night arrives. I just hope Surfer Boy turns up at the car park. He can't ring me, and I hope he turns out to be the reliable sort. Given the lure of some sexy time, I'm fairly confident that he'll show. I dress in black pants that are not too feminine from a distance, an ivory lacy top, and flat black shoes for the after walk. Around my head for a semi disguise, I wrapped a maroon-coloured silky scarf that I had stolen from one of the bitches at the factory when they dropped it in the locker room a few nights earlier. Packed into my black shoulder bag is an oversized black jacket with a hoody and my disguising reading glasses. The bourbon and Pepsi go in. Certain that I had plenty of codeine in the bathroom cabinet, I didn't go buy any more, but I can't find the old packet, the shops are shut so I'm forced to do without. A bit disconcerting given Byron is a much stronger fitter guy than Dave. At least I've paid more attention to the alcohol this time and it should be more effective depending on Byron's tolerance levels. Damn, the bag is heavy. I add my penknife. Last thing I slip into my purse is Dave's mouth refresher bottle. Just to add to the fervour.

ó

It's time to go. I kiss Stu goodbye, saying I'm going over to Melita's place and leave. I drive over to Terrigal and park a few streets back from the pub towards the beach. On the way over, I have visualised the scenario up at the cliff tops near the Skillion. I doubt I can convince Byron to climb over the safety barrier fence at the very top, so I'll lead him to another bare bit of high sheer cliff face to the north. Not as high but high enough to do the damage and I'm feeling pretty confident now with my plans.

I'm walking down to the pub carrying the bag over my left shoulder. I'm trying not to lean to the left but walk straight as if my bag is not as heavy as it is. I stop to wrap the bottles in the jacket to stop them clinking together. I get going again and as I approach; I notice no lights on at the pub. No noisy crowd on the balcony. Nothing. Then I finally remember its Easter Sunday and alcohol consumption and purchase is banned in our hypocritical so-called Christian society we have here. Sometimes I'm so dumb. I can't see the car park yet but I'm really hoping Byron is waiting there for his last big night with me. Only barely stopping myself from breaking into a run, I pass the building and step into the car park. One white commodore and one Surfer Boy leaning up against it exhaling smoke from a cigarette.

"Where's ya car?"

"A few streets back over there outside my girlfriend's

place."

"We were hanging out this afternoon and I can pick it up later from there, it's not far. I felt like the walk anyway."

I thought of saying I just got a taxi due to car problems or something but then he'd expect to see the taxi I came in. Plus, he might have been scared off that I wouldn't leave easily either after a hook up or if we didn't get along. I know you can just call a taxi anytime, but it can be a hassle the later it is after closing time. He lets the cigarette fall to the ground and rubs his foot around and smothers it. Grinding it into the ground. He must have been waiting a while.

"How is that we didn't even think about the Pub being closed?"

"Yeah, I guess we'll have to go back to mine then."

"Well, lucky for us I've bought along some bevvies. Bourbon and coke. Maybe we could go somewhere and watch the ocean in the moonlight."

"Yeah nah."

"Not really into that soppy sort of shit ya know."

Far out, I wasn't expecting that! I'm starting to think things are not going my way at all. First the pub shut and now this.

"I thought you would be because you like surfing and all."

"It's just my ex was always on about being romantic and crap all the time. She hated the fact I never bought flowers. She'd say I wasn't romantic enough and she'd always be lighting those candles everywhere and loved all those frigging feel-good messages. Plastered them all over her walls in her flat. It's just not me."

"I can't stand those waste of space moral message things too. They make me want to puke. I was in someone's house the other day and this couple had this in-your-face one in their kitchen. Glaring black writing on a wooden board with a white background so it really stood out. I couldn't look at it. It annoyed me too much. I just knew it would say some stuff that these two idiots don't do because I reckon, they are both bloody hypocrites."

I say this without fibbing this time. I try and keep my head framed in this like-minded space which is a bit of a struggle given the sexist attitude Bryon the Bigot is showing me.

"We could go and look at the moon and you could just think of me instead of her?" I tried again.

"It would just be a turn off."

Shit this bloke is a stubborn fuck.

"We could take your takeaways back to mine and sink em there? Not out there in the elements like. A bit of comfort ya know with a soft couch, that kind of thing. He says this while his eyes drop down my body and back up again."

"Okay." I hear myself saying. I have no back-up plan and I'm going to be willingly entering the den of a potentially volatile, maybe violent man. He wants one thing and when he works out that he's not going to get it, he'll probably be dangerous. I'm weighing up the risk and hoping I can adapt. As I get in his car, I'm imagining how if this bloke had showed respect and a genuine liking of women, of me, and wasn't the complete sexist shit that he is, the trajectory of the night could be me enjoying the attentions of a man in a normal sexual & companionable way like other people do all the time. I chose this one precisely for his bad attitude and I must go with what I've started I tell myself.

We don't speak on the way there. Cool by me. I'm rapidly thinking up what to do. At least try and get him paralytic as soon as I can. That's my plan so far. That was always my plan so yes, I'll stick with that, and I'll have to work it out as I go along. Adlib it. I'll try to disarm him and render him useless first up, that's the first aim. Glancing at his face, I feel a wave of superiority over him like I used to when in the same room as Vincent the fuck.

We drive over to North Avoca which is fine. I thought I'd have to walk back along the beach if he lived at south Avoca to skirt around the lake, but I won't have to walk that far to make it back to my car later. He drives us into a villa like complex of a few dwellings and I notice it's private from peering neighbours so that's alright. He parks the car outside the garage. I find myself looking and noticing the garage door. Either the wagon doesn't fit in the garage, he's filled the garage with stuff or he's too lazy to go in there with it. His house is frugal with furniture. I lug the bag in and lower it down next to the one wooden, pine chair pushed into a small matching round table he has in the open plan portion, next to the kitchen. The bottles clink loudly as I do this.

"Love that sound don't you Byron?"

"Yeah awesome."

"Have you got ice to cool down the coke?"

He points to the freezer.

Yeah fuck, I've got to do everything. This guy is no gentleman that's for sure. I suspect he's testing me to see if I'll be the whore slave mother that he wants from a relationship with a girl. Well, here's my little test buddy. Instead of getting the ice out, I pull out one of the Cougar bottles and the Pepsi, place them smack in the middle of the kitchen table and ask him where the toilet is. As I walk through his place, I take in everything trying to think up some scenario of suicide. After using the toilet, I quietly open his bathroom cabinet doors to see if he has any useful medication or drugs that would help knock him out. Panadol is all I see. That suggests he might have a high alcohol tolerance if that's all he usually takes. No way to know for sure but I'll have to go easy on the coke so the spirits is as concentrated as I can get it. No doubt he'll allow me to get his refills. That's a handy misogynous bonus for me.

I walk past a door that must lead to the internal garage. Back in the kitchen, Byron has placed two glass tumblers on the table, but the other ingredients are where I'd left them. No crystal for Byron, unlike Stefan. His tumblers I suspect are old jam jars. I dutifully crack some ice cubes onto the table and put them, some coke and then mostly Bourbon into one glass. Usually, people pour drinks the other way around but who cares. As I slide that across to where Byron is standing. Supressing my thoughts inside about this loser, I say a bit coyly,

"I'm sure you like it strong."
I make mine and explain how I don't need much and maybe it's due to my smaller body size. Mine is ice, mostly full coke with a smidgeon of bourbon. We move into the lounge room, and I find a chair separated from the main lounge. I must keep the sexual distance and just get him smashed. This is not going to be easy task given he's not a big talker.
"Where do you usually surf?"
"Oh, usually Avoca. Sometimes Wambi depending on the banks."
Silence. Shit I'm thinking. He's sipping so damn slow. Something salty should make him drink quicker.
"Have you got any chips or something?"
"Yeah, I do."
"Where are they? Don't get up I'll get them."
Top right cupboard above the microwave.
I find some corn chips. I look in the refrigerator for some cheese.
"Do you want some melted cheese on the corn chips?"
"Yeah awesome."
I noticed in the car I was starting to feel a bit hypoglycaemic from lack of food. Hot and quivery. Making this food will fix it and stall for more time. Taking the bottle back out to the lounge room, without asking, I pour some more Bourbon straight into his glass to the top. As I'm leaning over him, I slip him this tit bit,
"Call me weird, but it's a turn on for me watching hot guys drink, you know."
I go super slow slicing up the cheddar cheese block. Eating chunks as I go. Byron turns on the television to some footy channel. Every now and then, I'll go back out to Byron and say 'bottoms up' with a suggestive giggle. He drains his glass looking up at me and I pour more grog into it. No coke now. I'm grilling the corn chips when Byron walks a bit unsteadily to the bathroom letting rip a loud fart as he goes. What a charmer! I can then hear the tell-tale sounds he is on his way to inebriation with the tinkle continually stopping and starting. While he's in

there I find his room and look around for a thick sash or belt or something. I can't find anything. The toilet flushes and I'm already out of his room. The corn chips are starting to burn. I pull the tray out and flick the black ones off. I open a window and look for a fan switch to take away the smell. Byron grunts a bit and walks back out to the lounge. I notice his blue jeans are sagging below his butt crack now showing his jocks. Not an attractive look. But a good sign. He's starting to get a bit shabby. Just how I need him.

"When's the fucking food ready?"

There is a slight moment at the end of that where I'm sure he's about to address me with the name bitch, but he holds back like the great guy that he is.

I turn the griller off, and I go pour another straight one for him. He grunts again and then burps into my face. Yeah nice.

I'm starting to feel angry now. As I go back to the kitchen, I veer away to the closed door I saw before. Glancing back to make sure he's still watching television; I open the door and switch on the light to the garage. There's quite a collection of tools and stuff here. There's a narrow workbench and a rusted white fridge. I rummage through some draws in a steel cabinet. Electrical cords, drills, and finally I spot some rope. It's that blue and yellow Telstra rope. A long lot of rope. I'd prefer something wide, but I can't be fussy right now. With one end, I make a loop and small as I can, then I push the next bit of rope through the loop to make a slip knot. I pull enough through to make a loop about sixty centimetres in diameter. I gather up the rest of the rope and bring it into the kitchen and place it all under my bag with the loop on top.

I stand next to the griller and start eating the corn chips and cheese while watching the top of Byron's head as he watches the television.

"Come on with the bloody food woman!"

Pretty extreme bad behaviour considering this is like a first date and we hardly know each other. He must be pretty wasted to be treating me so badly so early in the relationship. What girl would hang around with that treatment? I go back out and pour more bourbon into his glass and tell him I'll just go get it now for him. I look at his face and I see Vincent's. Then in the next instant I see Byron's flushed red face. He's drinking that drink as I walk out. Yes, he must be super smashed now. That is a lot of alcohol he's drunk.

I pick up the rope and then rummage in my bag for Dave's spray bottle. Fingers round it I sniff it as I walk over behind Bryon slowly and spray it ever so lightly on his shoulders and hair. Already the odour permeates the lounge room, but Byron doesn't notice. Now I'm feeling pretty tense and worked up. I can't really describe it but there is a multitude of intense emotion swirling inside me. The rope is now in my hands with the loop spread out. I'm right behind Byron. I lean forward fast and drop the loop over his head and pull the end as fast as I can. His arms fly up and he tries to get his fingers under the rope. I lean back with one foot against the back of the couch for more leverage. I can see Byron's face reflected in the glass window in front of us. I see his eyes. I see anger then I see fear. His eyes widen. His whole body starts thrashing forward then sideways. He makes a groaning sound and the bare skin on the back of his neck starts to go dark and a bit purplish. It seems both ages and just moments that Byron struggles with me. I look at his reflected eyes and they change into blank. He has stopped fighting. He is here and now he's nothing. Doesn't exist. It's like a mini unfelt and unseen tornado has sucked up his soul and taken him up through the roof and away. I keep the rope tight and inhale the spray from his neck. My emotions shift from overwhelming red-hot anger to feeling completely in control and powerful. I have just cleaned the world of some stinking, dirty bad mess. For a tiny millisecond, I can see Debbie's smiling face.

6

I release my hold on the rope and pull the head back, so it

doesn't loll forward. I take my knife, and I go and stand in front. I just look at the body for a while. I pull back a sleeve and do a tiny cut to watch the ooze. I can't tell you what's running through my mind at this point. I can't remember. My hands are sore. Next thing I know I'm in the cold, concrete garage searching the walls, the ceiling, the floor, everything to help me devise a way to make him hang himself. There is an extendable aluminium ladder. Also, thick wooden rafters above me. How do I elevate this heavy body? To stop myself from becoming flustered, I decide to at least first get the body in there and then focus on the next part. If I'm actively doing stuff, then I can keep it all together and get this done.

Elbows bent under the armpits, I haul the body sideways and half onto the carpet. Stepping and leaning backwards I drag the body on its back across the floor and down the tiny concrete step into the garage. Wafts of bourbon and menthol permeate the stillness replacing the mustiness. A weird sensation is the complete emptiness to the space that was not there before. Emptier than before. The face is bulging outwards. Like it's growing.

I stop to let the body down in the centre of the garage. As I'm having a breather, I pull off a wide silver ring from Byron's finger and place it around my right thumb. That's the closest finger of mine it will fit. I flip the ladder over to make an A frame and lock in the fasteners. Lifting the ladder close to...not sure whether to call it a corpse yet. Or just a body? I always think of a disintegrating old body as a corpse. Never a warm one. Lifting it close to the body, I take the end of the blue and yellow rope I climb the ladder to near the top and throw it between the yellow pine beams above me. On the ground again I start pulling the rope at an angle. This is not working. Too heavy and the thin rope is cutting into my hands too much. I must keep calm. I'm glad this garage is so private. This is a lot less stressful than out in the open. I pull the rope again, but I can't keep the tension on. Looking around again, I walk clockwise around the garage opening more draws, the fridge and then I find under the workbench another rope that's long and thicker and made of that brown rough fibrous stuff. The work bench is fixed to the wall. I make a slip knot out of one end and push it under the back and under the armpits. Up the ladder, I thread it through the rafters. Then I take the end down to one of the work bench legs. Pulling from there, I can slowly lift the body up. I keep the tension on and wrap the rope a few times around the bench leg and then tie it off. I try the same with the other rope which is too hard on my hands. I find some thick welding gloves and that flattens the pressure on my palms. Pulling hard, it rises more, and I wrap the rope around the other bench leg and tie off. Then I untie the brown rope, lift more, and tie off. There is finally air between the shoes and the concrete floor. Continuing alternating ropes for I don't know how long, my arms start to quiver and ache. Satisfied the height is right and high enough now, I climb up the ladder, release the shoulders from the brown rope and leave the original one on. I position the ladder where it would look like Bryon would have comfortably stepped off it. I undo the rope ends from the bench legs, coiling the brown one and throwing it back under the table.

Turning now to face him, it's absolutely looking like suicide. Byron was depressed from losing his job and losing his girlfriend. He flagged his declining state of mind via text messages to family and friends before the actual night of his death. He drank way too much the night he took his own life. The bottles of bourbon and Pepsi can be seen in the kitchen and near the television. He placed a rope over his head, climbed the ladder in his garage, stepped off and hung himself. It's all there for everyone to see. Closing the door behind me but leaving the garage light on, I go into the bathroom and wash my hands. Cupping my pink palms, I drink from the tap. In the kitchen I take a tea towel, slightly wet it and wipe over surfaces that I've touched. In the lounge room, I take out my glass with the tea towel and wash it, dry it and place it in a cupboard, wiping as I go. I go and find my knife and rinse off the blood and use my fingertips to rub off the stubborn brown smears.

Taking a last look around, I check in my bag for all my stuff and leave, ever so softly, locking the front door behind me.

Unsure of the time, I guess its early morning. I find it quiet outside, no noises of traffic. A steady breeze is blowing in from the ocean filling my nostrils and cooling me down. Soon, I'm calmly and quickly walking along the middle of the darkened road back to my car. I walked along the middle of the road because that's how I felt. Like I owned it. Like I owned the world. I owned life. I owned death. I see no one, only a slender white and black cat stalking a larger, plumper, and uglier grey one in a driveway. I silently wish the slender cat good luck with its asymmetric quest.

O

Again, no media headlines of murder. Suicides are not often circulated as news unless they are people already in the public arena or there is something significant about it. I've pulled it off again even adapting to major unexpected changes to my original plan. It was after Byron that unfortunately I started to believe I was getting rather good at doing this stuff. I wish I had thought otherwise.

CHAPTER 18 NANNY AND PA

I THINK A LOT ABOUT THE END MOMENT.
Death. The transition from fully there and alive to absolutely
and completely gone. Never ever to come back and be alive
again. Warm, hot even and soft, then cool, cold, hard, and rigid.
Rigid like when you pick up a desiccated rat corpse by the tail
and the whole curved shape is retained to form an inflexible
sinewy coat hanger with tufts of grey fur.

◊

My first exposure to death was on my grandparent's farm. My
mother sent me there by train on my own, every holiday. She
was happy to offload me to Nanny. The sheep farm was in the
Riverina amongst the flat irrigated plains that drained into the
Murray River. The land carried sheep, rice, and soybean crops
in what seemed like big wide bedsheets spread over the entire
landscape. A much larger light blue sheet above us all was the
sky that was endless and stretched to infinity in every direction.
Everyone and everything lived in the bed in between. As a kid,

lying on my back down near the yabby dam, I'd sometimes pretend the earth was flat and I made up imaginary worlds beyond if you walked and walked in one direction past the clackety windmill and past the dusty ram paddock. That country's odour, smelt of diesel fumes blended with musty, earthy sheep droppings. Dry air and stubble.

I loved and hated the place. I loved the animals, and I loved/hated the eternal space. I often felt I didn't exist there and that I was merely an observer somehow, getting around as a ghost would. Making comments about things and people that no one could ever hear. No one heard me. Following people around with no response from them because they could not see me. The broad land made me feel insignificant, tiny and Nanny and Pa made me feel completely inconsequential.

Nanny treated me not as a treasured granddaughter but as an inept and fumbling farm hand that she was forced to endure. Nanny and my mother never got on. Nanny would see me, but she really would instead see my mum. It didn't help that my appearance is like mum. Same hair, eyes, shape of the face and all that. My mother's mini me. I am not at all like my mum in personality but that made no difference. She's disorganised, scatty, I would say illogical and often irrational. Her brother, my uncle is not like her either. He's more like Nanny. That may be why he is the golden boy in mum's family. He is my soft sand island in amongst an impenetrable paddock of blackberries and devil burr thorns that try to hurt you at every step. I'd love it when he'd visit the farm or on those rare occasions, home. He is how men should be. Friendly, warm, encouraging. An adult who never talked down to me but subtly boosted my feeling of equality and value. He is my benchmark for blokes. I measured and compared them all with him. As a kid and an adult, I could never get too much time with Uncle Dan, the man.

Nanny wore the pants and Pa followed suit on attitude towards me. His health also conspired against him to stop him from getting close to me physically. He was deaf and spruiked cranky dementia wherever he shuffled. I'd avoid him. I'd avoid Nanny too. She did have some impressive traits though. I did look up to her until my maturity questioned the reality of what I thought about the world as I started to figure out what is what and who's is who. A bit like when I realised religion is irrational and illogical and is a powerful cultural construct created and run by men to control all those weak and sad sucks out there.

All the farm animals were my friends except one of the chained up, black and tan kelpies that snarled when I came too close. Sometimes I felt all the other dogs, especially the Labrador and the chickens were my best friends on earth. We didn't have pets at home, and I became very attached to the farm animals. They never treated me like I was nothing as most humans did.

Around the farm there were always an animal to kill. Often, an animal met its death to feed us. This killing of my friends confused me, and I hated Nanny for it. I would spend hours and hours with the chickens poking bright green blades of grass at their beaks through the chicken wire, then letting them loose for their free-range exercise sessions and then herding them back into their dusty home with the help of the tan house Labrador dog. There were the old girls who lay the eggs and then there were the upstart young ones as Nanny called them. The upstarts we ate. Nanny taught me how to kill them so we could eat them. Initially, I'd watch her in horror, mesmerised as she'd cleanly severed off their heads over the red stump. No fuss. She'd cackle like a chook herself when sometimes she'd release her grip on the hen for her own amusement. The mass of white feathers ran around the grass spraying blood into the air from the gory neck where the head seconds earlier was connected. One time I picked up a head part to examine. It was narrow and flattened. I had never noticed this when these chickens strutted around alive. Once dead, the dark eyes shut with the crinkly red eyelids sealing the surface to something quite streamline, no longer letting in the world and sealing itself off as if sulking forever. At dinner, I would refuse to eat any of the chickens. Nanny would just cackle again but this time at me, not the chook. Over time though, after been directed by Nanny to kill them myself, I eventually ate them, but I always flinched when tiny feathers made it through the whole process and made it onto my plate.

Like the chooks and the dogs, I loved the sheep, but Nanny taught me how to position the lamb's warm bleating body against mine and slit their throats in one strong swipe of the blade. This ended up my job from early on. I still remember the first few times, observing myself from afar and feeling this raw shock at myself. A portion of me became mentally rigid, stiff, and completely unfamiliar. I gradually transformed into a hard-arse person just like Nanny, to allow me to get the job done. Eventually there was no adrenalin, I no longer felt nauseated, I would just change inside. Gradually, over some years I absorbed and accepted this different feeling of myself, this altered identity and thought it is really me, and not someone else. It made me feel strong and proud that I am not one of those weak squeamish people. However, I also felt conflict that there is no going back from the act that I did. It was me only, I am solely responsible for causing the whooshing away of that dead creature's spirit. Before a kill I would often momentarily mentally prepare and conjure up in my conscious the overall rigid hard arse me to enable myself to start and then complete the actions of killing. I detached myself from my bond with the lamb or the chicken. Other times, I don't remember even thinking at all. I just went through the motions and that was that. That's the easiest and smoothest way but also the most boring. It is always better to feel something.

The black crows banefully calling from the few huge gums on the farm were also my mates. Hearing them now always transports me back to that brown desolate place and I smell diesel fumes. I always admired the birds' intelligence. They constantly outwitted Pa. For some reason, I still do not know why, the satiny crows would regularly glide into the garden area in front of the bull-nosed veranda, but only when Grandpa sat in the centre of the raised pavilion. To me it seemed like the crows were on my side and deliberately taunted Pa by swooping in and around him with a cacophony of calling and flapping of their big black shiny wings. Their antics immediately set him off in a frenzy of obscenity shouting and arm waving. He'd keep his .22 rifle on the floor of the pavilion most days so he could take pot shots of things like the enormous goanna that kept stealing the chooks' eggs and would occasionally risk slinking across the lawn. After the old man's arm waving, the crows would go next level with the commotion becoming extra loud until the old man stepped out from under the shelter with the gun and started shooting at them. In an instant, they were gone. Never did any die. I tried once to tell Grandpa how he could make friends with them with offerings of meat chunks. He roused on me for wasting good food, obviously preferring them as adversaries.

ᕦ

This killing continued from early days at the farm to my adult role as a veterinarian nurse. For some reason, the vets always left it to me to euthanize the dogs, cats and any injured native wildlife that presented at the business and was deemed in need of death. Many young greyhounds not required anymore for racing would end up on our cold steel surgical table. We would drain their sleek bodies of lifesaving blood needed for blood transfusions for people's beloved pet dogs before they were destroyed. I hate that term, destroyed. I've heard of native villages in the world often having one revered individual person who has this destroyer type role. Their unique 'asset' is their detached aptitude to do any necessary killing the community needs. It appeared to me that I was this individual within the veterinary firm I worked for.

The greyhounds were routinely steered into the building through the rear door by weaselly old Mister Harold. He always wore his dog poo brown, sloping newsboy cap, looking like he'd come straight from the track. Dog after dog after elegant dog walked through that door. He would keep bringing them in for me to kill and I'd see him quietly take his wad of cash from my boss in exchange for their life blood. Every single one of these dogs behaved beautifully with me and this gnawed at my insides. Until I could no longer take it anymore and I resigned.

These affectionate hounds reminded me of the farm dogs and my other childhood friends, the chickens, and lambs that I was instructed to kill as a child. The repeated strain of mentally blocking out and detaching from them all became too much for me. The regret and guilt of taking their life surfaced too many times. I'd often picture the greyhound I was about to euthanise, resting contently on someone's couch in a loungeroom with their lanky front legs all outstretched. That is how their lives should have played out and could have played out.

Not a lot of things got to me back then, but the dogs did. They would send a thread to my heart and connect to me piercing through my surrounding force-field barrier that usually kept sweet entities like them wholly sealed out. Their powers of penetration would hit my protective response button, and I would not be able to act on their behalf and save them. This made me frustrated and angry, but I did not realise that this was what was happening. A similar feeling was with Debbie. I could not help her, so I felt extremely frustrated, and my anger built up. I suspect because I never recognised why I felt that way, that is the reason I failed later to stop my horrific ways and change.

CHAPTER 19 PLANNING AGAIN

THE UP FROM DOING BYRON DID NOT LAST LONG.
It was April and almost immediately I started planning again.
This was shit. Byron was supposed to be the last one. Too many
arrogant Vincents seem to come my way to feed my obsession
or compulsion or whatever you want to call it.

○

I compared the variables from my past efforts. What I liked
about the indoor staging of suicide is the fact that I can enjoy
the whole thing for longer. Out in the open with Dave, there
was the stress of people pulling into the car park and just simply
seeing us both there. My main apprehension was if a witness
sees there were two people there and not one. Communities can
be small, and circles can be tight. Any talk about a second person
present could be potentially mentioned to someone who is
relevant and then there is your initial seed of doubt about suicide
planted out to the public. Suicide assumptions transform to an
investigation of staged suicide-homicide. It's best to prevent any

ideas at all from the very start of any possible homicide. Let the scene say, just another suicide so no extra work to be done on this one. There is this paradox. My aim was to alert the public to the slackness of attitude in dealing with suicides but equally I did not want to be caught. The phenomenal catch for me which I only realise now is that to show the depth of investigatory flaws and the high potential of success of suicide staging, I would have to draw attention to all the suicide staging I have done. These staging deaths would then be investigated by law enforcement as homicides and then I could be caught. I do not want to be caught that's for sure. Any TV show that presents anything to do with prisons, freak me out and I cannot watch any of it. Kind of, too close to the bone.

Anyway, back to the choice of indoor stage or outdoor stage, I decided to go for a third indoor one. There is an intimacy inside a house with the privacy shrouding it all, that I crave. No one else around to interfere with the whole flow of it. It is much easier to stay focused and enjoy being in control with way less risk that the tables could turn by an incoming individual that could completely wreck it all.

A third different suicide method that I can stage indoors, I found difficult to work out. To stick to my plan of staging different suicide modes, I really should have chosen an alternate outdoors one to do say, the cliff jump or something else. Because I could not get out of my head the acute closeness to the skin and the bare muscles and the blood vessels of Stefan and Bryon, I wanted to experience that again. Indoors it would be. So, I decided on a repeat of the carbon monoxide type, but inside a garage. My reasoning was that the variable of indoor exhaust is different enough from outdoor to be worthy of another valid example of how people can stage. A mental note here was to ensure the next bloke lived somewhere with a private and contained garage and that he uses it to park his car. A junk filled garage, or a carport would fail the criteria. He obviously must have a car too.

Where to find such a fellow? As a precaution that I failed to follow through with last time, I thought I'd make sure I go further away from home and head north for more distance from my regular home orbit. This time I would find a club with poker machines and see if I could use the ideas that I formed from what Rocky had said. That ploy has been on the backburner since I found Byron at the beach. This next one I would try and find either at the Bateau Bay Pub or Diggers at The Entrance, about an hour drive away. This meant I'd more likely find someone who lives up that way and their house would be in that vicinity too.

The more pressure building up that I felt, the more I knew I had to take more precautions because I was more likely to become lapse with details if I could not concentrate properly. Further-a-field would put space between me and the next 'suicide'. Again, I began to feel in control again. Planning would ease my stress to some degree.

CHAPTER 20 STEREOTYPES

ONE MIGHT EXPECT SOMEONE WHO HAS KILLED people to fit a certain stereotype. Features of what people think they know about killers seem to saturate the crime shows on television, movies, and crime fiction novels. Not all people fit into all those neat and contained little boxes. The main outlying aspect about me is my gender. Most known people who do this stuff are men. Of course, there are some women but not many who take multiple lives. Of the females that do manage more than one, it is usually the loser nurses who poison their patients, who I would surmise feel extremely insecure and lacking power in their worlds. They administer drugs through a needle or a drip to completely helpless and vulnerable elderly people and babies that cannot retaliate. To me these killer nurses are supreme sad sucks. The people they euthanize usually have loved ones and friends even if they are old and, on the way out. What is the point in doing it? Besides the power trip, the only thing I can think of here is maybe they are bored at work. They feel smug and perhaps it's the annoying patients that are selected to go. Male nurses do this too. One in Germany was caught by authorities and thought to be the biggest modern mass killer for that country. There was a female nurse in the 1800s who would cuddle up to the patients in their beds as they died, in a kind of perverted unfettered emotion. Maybe she was different to the modern ones of today. I suspect she probably enjoyed the actual dying bit rather than briskly striding from the room to avoid detection after depressing down that death needle. Or who knows, maybe she is not different but is the female killer norm and it is cultural perception that drives the unemotional picture of female nurse killers. We will never know the answers to what most of these killers experienced at an emotionally level.

○

Seduction I find difficult. It is a tool expected to be the norm for a female killer of men. This does not come naturally to me even with my voluptuous chest. If it did, perhaps I would have kept going for longer or done over more in a shorter time. Or maybe it is a protective attribute where it forms a kind of a check to my activities, slowing me down so I don't trip up and get caught because I must analyse my actions and not take anything for granted.

Sometimes seeing bimbos working a bloke in a pub or nightclub makes me envious that they are so carefree about what they are doing. Other times I despise them thinking they probably don't even enjoy the sex they have invested their entire night for. They are losers that just want attention from men because they are so insecure, and it does not matter what attention it is. Lack of a father figure probably features highly. Some pitiful try-hard women fake multiple orgasms to help the men to get off. This effort is all for the benefit of the man. Maybe he is a total stranger they had just picked up and he's drunk twelve schooners of beer and now wants the root but having had or that beer, he's having a load of trouble performing or falls straight to sleep. Why women go through that crap I can't fathom. Plus, these blokes will just call them a slut and have zero respect for the girl anyway, so it is a huge mystery to me.

One nightclub I went to I remember there was a large

rectangular dance floor with floor space of a few meters wide, right the way around it. Mostly girls danced on the dance floor and there was a line-up of guys surrounding the floor three guys thick and these men just stood there still, just staring at us. No bopping to the beat or anything. That vibe was pretty gross. That is when you feel like you are a vacant slab of meat at the market ready to be picked, poked, and then discarded.

CHAPTER 21 POKIES PUB

I KEPT ON WITH MY NEW PLAN. IN CHOOSING CAR exhaust again for the stager component, all the details of parts I needed for that were already in my head from the first one. I made gear changes though. Instead of a one size doesn't fit all hose pipe, I decided on a rubber sink plunger. From this I can remove the handle and using a boxcutter, slice a hole in the rubber to fit the garden hose. If I made the hole smaller, then the hose should stay put once I forced it through the hole. Enough gas will flow through from one exhaust outlet I figured, if the car has multiple exhaust pipes. Enough gas to make a reading from a blood test is all that is probably required for evidence of using carbon monoxide in a solid attempt at self-euthanasia. Does not have to be enough to kill because the actual cause of death will be strangulation again. That works. I will try getting loser-man drunk, drugged, and unstable, somehow make them stagger to the garage, do the strangle struggle using a wide belt and then set up the staging components of them inside their car. All suggesting he had tragically given up on life. A few suicidal mobile phone texts to people too would add some nice emotional 'evidence'.

These plans never seem to work down to the detail though.

In the end, the cause of death changed from strangle to suffocation. Lessons I learnt included the value of a flexible mind. Once again though, I stuffed up.

6

It was September now. The time has come. I had the new stuff I needed including bourbon again. At least I thought I had everything. I had sourced another struggle belt. A nice wide and strong white, plastic affair I chanced on at the local Charity shop but stupidly forgot to pack it and failed to realise till way later. I had bought more codeine fortified Panadol too, but I forgot this also. My handbag was huge and heavy, but I could not do much about that. My black slacks this time had a deep pocket in which I could store my spray and new penknife. As a precaution, during one of my more anxious and paranoid days, I took my old trusty penknife with me to the beach and dropped it in a bin as I walked across a car park with my surfboard. A smaller, neat foldup knife from a seedy pawn shop in Gosford replaced it. I was sad to say goodbye to the original one. I had an attachment to it. Sentimental I suppose. I hate sentimental crap in others, and I really hate it in myself. Does everyone have these dumb internal contradictions or is it just me?

I told Stu my cover story. The week before I'd told work that I wasn't available till the following Wednesday. It was a Monday night this time. I thought a Monday is the optimal night to find a bludging loser that is too lazy to work. Heading north, I still had not decided on the place I'd try and find someone. As it turned out, I accidently missed both turnoffs to the Bateau Bay Pub. Thinking it was for the best that I put more safety distance between this next one and the past ones, I kept driving on to The Entrance.

Diggers Club rested on a crest along the main road north. Instead of pulling into the car park, I did a u turn at the nearby roundabout and doubled back the way I had come. Three streets along, I turned off the main road and drove towards the lake. I knew there was path running along the lake and I could use that to walk back to my car later. Cameras may be in the big open car park of the Club and that I wished to avoid. Thinking about this I made a mental note to try and leave the premises separately to the bloke I found inside, so I would not be seen leaving with him and then be later linked by authorities.

Lugging my oversized handbag and walking fast, I avoided the main road until the last street that led up to where the club is. I entered at the main entrance and filled out false temporary membership details on the paper slip the management asked for as you entered. First things first, I found a lady's room and freshened up my makeup. Then I wandered around until I saw the poker machine room. I bought a Lemon Lime and Bitters from the bar nearest the pokies and then slowly walked down each isle, subtlety checking out who was in there while simultaneously pretending to study the different machines before I chose one to play. Two women sat on stools in one aisle and three men were spaced apart amongst the rest of the machines. Two of the men were over sixty but one looked promising at about thirty years old. I settled on a chair in the same aisle as him, at the opposite end and gave him a polite smile as I sat down. He smiled back. This gave me confidence this latest 'project' would work for me. All I had to do was remember the prepared questions I needed to ask him about whether he had a car and find out how private his garage is. Then I'd persuade him to drive me back to his place. Not so easy for a girl who does not get around picking up guys all that often, well never really. I glanced over and he was already checking out my busty 'tits'. My top exposed some generous curves so that's to be expected I guess; however, it is all in the manner they do it. This guy was not that subtle and more on the lurid side. Good sign. His arrogance inflamed me. Yes, this man is what I am after, I remember clearly thinking.

CHAPTER 22 LEERS

THE LEER KEPT COMING AT ME FROM THIS BLOKE.
Pretending to be there to gamble, I started slotting coins into
the gleaming brightly coloured poker machines. Try as I might
to get that glazed-over appearance people get while sitting there
pulling the handles on these things, I just could not perfect it.
Too hyped. This did not deter leery at all. It seemed like hours
but was probably minutes, Leers cashed in his money from his
machine and left with his wallet, bestowing upon me one of
those disgusting patronizing winks only a certain type of sleaze
bag can do. I tried my best to smile coyly back like some pathetic
little girl. Because I was concerned, he was leaving for the night,
I most probably looked overly interested in him and this turned
out in my favour but not his. Wanting to get up from my seat
and try and see where he went but not wanting to look keen, I
managed to stay put and feed the machine some more. Out of
the corner of my eye, there he was, sauntering back. I did not
look up but stared dully straight ahead in front of me like a true
gambler. He strode closer, until he was right next to me carefully
placing a Lemon Lime and Bitters next to my coin stash on the
machine.

"Here you are, thought you might like this. He pulled over

a high stool and sat down."

"Ah gee, thanks, aren't you a darl. How did you know?"
As you can see, I am not so good at this chat up stuff. My memorised list of questions I needed to ask him burst into my head, and I nearly blurted them out right there and then without any prelude. Luckily, I got a grip and said something else instead.

"I haven't got a car."
Again, I am so hopeless at this social stuff, but it could have been worse. I try some more.

"I mean I've had a rough day because my car got totalled this morning and that's why I'm here wasting the money I don't have, to fix it on the pokies. Smart hey!" I fumble.
At least I was most probably debasing myself down to his level of life I am thinking. Losers gravitate to other losers.

"Were you alright?"

"Alright? I'm fine what do you mean?"

"With your car getting written off, you know."

"Oh that, yeah someone crashed into it while it was parked in the street. I wasn't in it."
Venturing another question, I asked,

"Do you ever do the pokies when you've had a bad day?"

"Sometimes, sometimes not."

"I just like to come here to wind down after work sometimes you know, have a few schooners, maybe dinner. It's not too busy during the week so I like that."
He is sounding like a single bloke which fits for me.

"Oh, what kind of work do you do?"

"I work in a hardware."

"Do you live round here then?"

"Yeah, a few streets over that way."
He pointed his arm in some direction, but I can't decipher where exactly he means from inside the club. Doesn't matter, as long his place is in walking distance back to my car is what I need. Tick to that part.

"Far enough away to drive here though?"

"Yeah, I'm not gonna walk, bugger that caper."

"So, no one to go home to or is this place an escape from

family?"

"No, no, no one at home. I live by myself. Just haven't found the right sheila yet. Moved in before and hasn't worked out so I'm not in a hurry with that caper."

By now I'm kicking myself about leaving the question about the configuration of the garage till right now. Why didn't I think this through like the rest of the planning and preparation? Dumb, dumb, and dumb I am. How the hell do I broach that one? I think how I have been able to ad lib before and change the plan, even change major parts like modes and locations and I am still here and not in jail. Problem is change adds tremendous risk. After doing each one, I spend a lot of time in my head going through the whole thing to work out if I had left anything out or in that will be my downfall. I am more likely to slip up if I have failed to plan for it.

Sipping my drink, I study his face. This guy looks about thirty but seems much older. Leers should be established in his job at his age.

"So, are you a pleb in the hardware or high up or something?"

"Not a shit kicker nah, I'm the manager."

"Does that mean you earn heaps for a nice house?"

He probably thinks I am sizing him up for a relationship and seeing if he has money and that gold digging thing. Little does he know what I am really sizing him up for.

"Oh yeah, my house is flash enough, at least that's what people tell me."

Obviously trying to impress me now.

"Roller doors on the garage then? I asked while laughing to soften the question.

"Not quite that, but it has doors", he said laughing along.

"As long as it has doors." I said nodding.

"Doors to keep your car in."

"It's got that yep."

He has no clue how I am really being sincere here. It is these secret parts of the 'action' or 'hunt' or whatever you want to call this part of the process, that I find somehow empowering.

Deluding them. The fact the garage has doors says to me it is enclosed and therefore private enough. It will not matter if it is connected to the house or stand-alone providing the car goes in, and no one can see what happens inside.

"Or do you have all your stuff in there instead of the car?"

"The cars in there."

"I guess you wouldn't want to leave a car out around Long Jetty."

"It's not too bad round here but yep, the car is safer in the garage for sure."

"Perhaps you should show me this plush place you have?"

"Um yeah righto, when?"

"Well now if you like, it'll save me from throwing my money down the neck of this machine."

"Okay. I'm Shane by the way", he said, his hand outstretched for me to shake.

"Audrey", I said as I shook his hand smiling.

He has this kind of quivering nervy look in his eyes I had not seen till now.

"I'll meet you in the car park in a sec, just gotta visit the ladies first."

This gives me some stalling time to try and have so we don't depart the building together or even at the same time. The less link up the better. I can't do much about the car park though. Inside the toilet, I lock the door and check my bag and go through all the stuff I have. I check my pocket in my trousers for the mouth spray and my knife. All there. I still do not notice the belt and pills are not there. These two items are fundamental to the plan, and I do not even notice they are missing. I must be flustered. If only I had realised this big mistake, and the mission might have been aborted. A waft of spray hits my nostrils, and I find myself feeling instantly alert and energetic. After laying some more lippy around my mouth, I head on out. Leery is waiting near his car. A silver Camry sedan. As I walk over, I glance at the exhaust. Just the one, cool. Casually I get in and as I sit next to him, part of his neck is exposed and I notice one of those wanky, gold chains encircling his neck. Not thick like those druggy gangster types but still a chain that says to me he thinks a bit too highly of himself. This might sound sexist, but necklaces are truly for women only not men. They do nothing to make men look better or attractive. Chains on men are a symbol of ego in my book. We drive through the streets and soon into his cement driveway. He paused in front of the detached garage, climbs out, unlocks, and rolls up the door. I climbed out after he does this with my bag and then he parks inside. We walk outside and after closing the doors, we go inside his house. The glimpse I get of the garage internals is promising. Completely private. No vast windows or viewpoints into it from the outside. And bonus, it is not too far from the house. I hear my stomach rumbling as he shows me into the kitchen.

"Whoa, I heard that", says Leers.

For a weird moment he looked like he wanted to put his hand on my tummy as if I was pregnant. Repulsed, I turn around leaving my back for him to look at and open the first draw I could find in front of me. I have no idea if I hid my feelings from my face or not.

"Got anything to eat round here?".

"Um yeah".

"Nothing fancy, just toast will do. Something simple to shut my belly up."

Leers opens another cupboard and pulls out a loaf of bread and puts some in the toaster on the bench.

"Ham and cheese do? or I've got some leftover pizza?"

"The ham and cheese please. I'll just do a tour if you don't mind while you sort dinner out."

"You'll have to excuse the mess. I don't bring people home all that often."

"That's fine."

I wander through the house and can tell that what he has said so far, seems to match up. No photos around of a previous family or kids or anything. Pretty much a single bloke from what I can glean. Some houses have a feminine touch to the furnishings. The artwork will be soft and matching, little nick knacks here and there will be completely ornamental pieces that have no purpose except aesthetics. Soft curtain patterns. These details tell of a woman having lived in the house. In contrast, a man's house might have mismatching items, art. Bolder furnishing patterns and colours and no frilly stuff. Items around are useful ones. Not much else. Leer's house had zero woman's touch. No pets either.

Walking back into the kitchen, I ask him if I can get a drink.

"Yep, I'll get you one. What would you like? Beer or bourbon? Sorry I haven't got wine or anything."

"Let's have bourbon."

Perfect, his bourbon first then mine. My mind turns to fast tracking the alcohol consumption to turn down the muscle power on this bloke.

"Good idea Audrey."

"I like mine strong, do you like yours strong?"

"Sure do."

He takes a deep sip from his glass as he hands me mine. He stares at me and his grinning leery thing spreads across his face. This annoys me so I tell him to take over with the food while I sit down. Stupid of me I know because I do want him to be thinking of me like that but also, I hate it. Instead of being nice to him, I say some mean stuff.

"So, what exactly is wrong with you that you don't have a girl? You are what, forty something and not hooked up?"

"I'm actually thirty-eight thanks, and as I said to you before, I haven't met the right one."

I grin back at him especially now that he is showing offense at my words. I wondered whether it was the age bit or the girl bit that cut. I offer him a way to dig a hole. His own one.

"Yeah, there are so many scrags round here that treat guys like absolute crap that you are better off without them really."

He does not reply so I give him another shovel.

"Why would any guy want to live 24/7 with some bimbo that orders you around in your own home telling you what you should do, wear this, wear that?"

"Exactly. They think they are something when they are just

not. I don't need that."

"Yeah Shane, I used to know this girl and what she'd do is slime her way into these guy's lives and tease them constantly with her tarty looks. She would without fail have some excuse not to have sex with these poor bastards while pushing them to buy her expensive jewellery and clothes until they finally started to get the shits with her. Just as they started to jack up, she would dump them big time, stopping all contact with them. Then, she'd be onto the next poor bloke. And of course, she would keep all the dosh she'd siphoned out of them all."

"That is completely fucked. Yep, that bitch needs to be taught a lesson. Women need to understand what they are. Dumb arses the lot of them. Well except for maybe one percent like…like you."

I look at him and laugh. He is getting worked up a bit and doesn't realise he's the one that needs the lesson and he's going to get it. He's going to get it from a dumb arse too. The more he talks like that the easier the whole action bit is for me.

One thing I must decide on though is how I get Leers into the garage. It is a little way from the house. The one thing that I know works, is the strangulation in the chair but there were only the car chairs in that garage. No others. Not a lot of room in there either. I am having doubts I can convince him to get in the driver's seat and sit there but I'm going to have to try. Even if he becomes highly inebriated, I suspect he would become a stubborn shit and not do anything I suggest. It's because I doubt that he has spent enough time in relationships learning the give and take with it all. He has become too independent and insular and therefore not the team player. Bachelor bros are probably his only mates. He is someone not easily manipulated, not even for the pussy lure.

I'm thinking I could maybe risk moving him in the open over to the garage afterwards. Either a drag or maybe there is a wheelbarrow or something. But no that won't work because his body needs to get the gas in it before he's dead. Anyway, that might be way worse if someone saw. At some point I walked over the lounge room windows and looked outside. I noticed it was becoming pitch black outside. No main streetlights shining over his house.

We sit down in his lounge room to eat the food. I am so hungry. Bolting the food down, I then go and pour more drinks making Leers' drink, highly potent. He puckers his mouth slightly as he tastes it. I smile at him leaning forward a bit showing a bit of big cleavage and laughing inside at the hypocrisy of it all. Leers gives me his leer. Love it. I start talking about the swine flu and asked him if he is scared now that someone in Australia has died. Weird, I remember asking him this but cannot remember anything else about the conversation. I do remember thinking it would be easy for him to stock up on survival gear from his work. If he became hard core, he could be bringing bits and pieces home every day, like food storage buckets, masks, disposable overalls, gum boots one can sterilise easily, chemicals. If it were me working there and I became freaked out about the end of days, I know I'd be getting all the gear very, very cheap.

Now and then I do have these memory lapses, but I don't know why. I doubt it is an alcohol induced memory loss because I get them when I'm not drinking at all or only had a small amount. I managed to hardly drink that night although I made it look like I drank a fair amount. Drinking just enough to take the edge off.

I could feel my energy levels rising while we sat there in the lounge room. I stood up and pulled the curtains closed as we talked. Questions about me I smoothly deflected. As I did more of these Vincents, my patience grew less and less with the lead up.

Ó

It is time I really figure out how to get Leers over to the garage. I am thinking I could keep pressing him with the bourbon so he's paralytic or spike his drink with medication, so he collapses enough for me to drag him out. Not ideal. I discretely check my

bag for the box of Panadol Forte and finally realised I had not
bought it along, so I excused myself for the toilet again and went
to check his cabinet. I left him with another strong one while I
checked out the bathroom. A quiet rummage revealed nothing
useful at all. Flushing the toilet for cover, I came out. I decided
I would give him a test to see how pliable he would be to me
later asking him to go to the garage. If he agreed to move chairs,
in the house, I figured he would be primed in his head to move
again when I asked him. Either that or he is going to be that
stubborn bastard I suspect he is. If so, I seriously doubt I will be
able to follow through with my plan of making sure I leave him
that night with carbon monoxide in his blood.

"Why not sit in my chair?"
This was awkward because he was in a two-seater so the
expectation would be for me to sit next to him.

"Yeah, how come?"

"It'll be cosier you know."

"Dunno."

He did not seem very drunk to me. Not slurring his words
enough. His face was reddening but that was about it. Thing is,
I really could not be bothered with the prelude part any more
with this bloke. I stood behind my chair and leaned over patting
it while smiling at him coyly. I then patted my pocket and felt
the lump of my knife and spray. I pulled out the spray and jetted
some into my mouth and deliberately fumbled with it so I could
accidently spray the chair.

"I know! How about I give your neck and shoulders a
massage over here. Just to loosen you up. When was the last time
you've had a massage, I bet ages?"

"Righto, alright you win, I can't remember the last time."
As he sits down where I want him, I walk back to his chair to
get his drink and hand it to him as his little reward.

"Finish that and I'll just pour you a fresh one before I start."
I hand him the next one, he chugs down half of it. Finally, he is
seated with his head and neck bent forward and I am standing
squarely behind him. I do not actually want to touch this guy but
what persuades me is the extra shock he'll get the more relaxed

he is. So, I push my hands into his neck and start kneading his hard flesh. The gold necklace was in the way, so I pressed either side of it. He is groaning, head down and starting to relax. I can feel he is giving into the moment and sensation.

"How does that feel?"

"Yup gaate."

I think I might now have him with the sound of that slurring.

"That's good. Here, have some more bourbon to relax those muscles more."

I hand him his drink to finish. Then I am thinking I had better scan outside before we move from the house to the garage. That is if he's going to move.

"Just a sec."

I walked away and cracked open the door to the outside slightly and stood silently listening and looking. Very still outside and very dark now. Any moon for the night had not yet arisen. No traffic noises or dogs.

"How bout we maybe do some sexy stuff you know?"

I remember trying to say this in a super sultry voice, but it came out all micky mouse to my ears. Didn't matter.

"Orr yer."

"One little thing though Leers."

I could not believe I slipped up so badly, actually saying out loud what my internal voice says by calling him 'Leers"!

"One little thing ears," I tried to cover.

"I can only do sexy stuff in cars."

No response, so I kept on.

"Your car is perfect. That backseat will be so cute. All nice and private in there. You'll see."

Reaching for his hands, he slurs something I take to be a yes. Relieved and excited, I haul him up to his feet and he lurched sideways and nearly takes us both to the floor. A shuffle and he rebalances while I put a sensual arm around his waist and imagine him to be some pumping hot bod instead of Leery the loser man, clone of Vincent. Little steps and we are out the door along a short path and into the garage. I shove the garage door up as Leers leans onto the wall. After guiding him in, I pull down the door after us. Dark seclusion. Leers switches on the garage light as we move around his car. It is a tight squeeze, but I manage to manoeuvre him around the bonnet and alongside the right side of the car and into the back seat, kind of headfirst and half in. He does not move so I leave him like that with his face into the seat.

I look in the ignition and no keys. Shit! They are not in the car. My whole plan could fall in a heap if I do not find those keys. I close my eyes for a moment and focus on staying calm. Just as I am doing that, I can hear a siren blaring along the nearby main road and becoming louder. Not moving a muscle, I wait. The siren dissipates into the distance, and I can breathe again. I must go back into the house to get the keys.

This was a time not to be seen by anyone and an idea came to me. I really cannot afford to be seen, but Leery can be seen. I looked around the garage. Then, scanning the car, I see in the backseat, half underneath Leer's frame, a big, branded, work jacket from the hardware. Plus, there is a baseball style cap from some footy club down in the foot well. Leers was lying on the jacket, so I slowly pulled it from under his head and shoulders without disturbing him from his alcoholic slumber. Absolutely no flinch. He is well and truly out of it. I put his bulky jacket on, folding the corners of the collar onto my neck, and gathered my hair up and tucked it under the footy cap. My slacks being black and not too tight blended into the overall masculine Leery look. Moving all gorilla man-like I walk along the dark path and into the house. Searching the house looking for the car keys I find them on the kitchen table.

I get back to the garage and then realise I'd forgotten my hui kit (aka huicide kit) so I again walked like a bloke back to the house, grabbing my handbag and holding it to my tummy as I walked back across to the garage. Its feeling risky to keep going back and forth in the open, no matter how dark it is or how much I look like Leers but looking at him makes me feel calm. He is just how I want him.

It is time to sort out the exhaust. I cut a hole in the rubber piece and forced the garden pipe through it. Sounds dumb I know but I had not thought through this critical part of the process. I must have been focusing on the engine being running for long enough to get substantial amounts of exhaust toxins into the car interior and into the body. The exhaust pipe will heat up to burning hot. I was fixated on the whole attachment melting off and the garden hose falling out. The hose goes into the rubber funnel but how the hell do I fit that funnel to the bloody exhaust pipe, so it won't just come off? Swearing at myself, I pace around the garage. I find some metal chain in a toolbox and a shackle in a white ice cream container full of odd bits of screws, nails, and other useful men's junk just waiting for the day it gets to do something. Lucky but not lucky for me this works. The flange of the rubber is floppy and wide enough to overlap the exhaust pipe by a good length. I wrap the chain around and around and secure it tight with the shackle through two links. I push the hose pipe into the exhaust in a fair way and test the firmness of it all. The whole hose has ample length to fit through the open door along the back seat and down Leer's throat. I place it over him and level with his head.

This is it. I am all set. I hope this works. I go to pull out the belt from my bag that is sitting on the concrete floor for the ultimate action, but it is not there. Remembering the gear check at Diggers, and I realise I could not see it then. Standing there I stare down at Leers. Maybe I don't need the belt with him face down and him passed out like he is. First looking over to check the garage door in tightly shut, I reach into the front of the car and turn on the ignition. I turn it off again. There is a rag like large square of cloth over on the ground. I go and pick it up and try and secure it over my mouth. Then I turn the car back on. I climb in over Leers and twist his head to the side and then place the hose into his mouth. I stick my fingers in there to part his teeth. Wiping the salivary yuck on his shirt, I force the stiff tube further in. He starts to move and does some spluttery thing, so I pull it out slightly. It might be his gag reflex the pipe prodded. Pulling it back a bit settles him. I hold the whole lot in position while he sucks in the toxic gas. Now and then he moves so I reposition the tube. Problem is instead of each movement sequence becoming weaker and weaker, he is becoming stronger.

My priority is to force as much carbon monoxide into his system for as long as I can hold him. I start to feel dizzy. At one point I leave everything and get out of the car. Sitting down for who knows how long I am having trouble thinking. Eventually I recover enough to reposition the rag and lucky I do this because as I stand up Leers pushes the tube out of his mouth. Quickly, I turn off the car and then I get in there on top of Leers and force his head back down into the chair. Using all my weight on him and getting a grip with my right leg onto the back of the front chair, I keep his mouth completely flush into the surface of the seat. Some more thrashing but not hugely forceful. That slows and I push his head back to the side so I can see one of his eyes. His movements stop and then he does a sort of last ditch fit like the chickens in their final throes of life. I must push him down and hold on again and stretching my leg back into the chair. Again, he stops, and I can lean forward, move his head, and see his eyes. I see the rush of life come out of him. His eyes become still.

Without looking at my pocket, I pull out my new little penknife and pull up his sleeve. Not sure why but again I feel like I must test out the dead flesh. Watch it ooze. It gives me this powerful feeling to see the sharp blade cut into the body. I would love to cut in further but somehow resist the urge. Cutting him risks failing the overall staging of suicide that I am attempting to present to the world.

ტ

Ideally, I would like to do a cut into the masculine bicep, both before death and one after. Might sound crazy but I could not do that to someone. That is torture in my book. People describe Jack the Ripper as especially cruel and vicious because he disembowelled his victims and removed various bits and pieces from their bodies. I think he was humane, for a killer. He slit their throats fast and their deaths would have been quick and relatively low stress and low in pain. Just like what you strive to do with farm animals, aiming to minimise their stress. All the gruesome activity was done after the women were dead, so they themselves never felt or suffered any of it. This is of course unless they were floating above and watching down at their dead carcasses, but even then, presumably, they would not have felt any pain.

6

To add to the staging of this one I had planned to send suicidal text messages. A bit of a mix between the text messages I sent from Byron's phone seeding the idea of suicide into the minds of his closest friends and family, and the suicide message I wrote and left in Stefan's house. Byron had told me about losing his job and splitting with his girlfriend. These facts meant I could easily put that depressing information out there to support the suicide staging. These two variables of losing your job and losing your partner are widely known as substantial risk factors for suicidal people. Leers did not seem to have any obvious problems like that so I would have to formulate a suicide note that tells people what possessions they receive like I had planned to do for Stefan. Only with Stefan, I lacked enough knowledge of his possessions to formulate a list that I could be confident with.

First, I must find the phone. I look in the car, and in his pockets but it is not there. It is not in the car so it must be in the house. I did not see it with the car keys but then the last time I go back into the house, I find it in the corner of the kitchen bench. Few possessions in his house so not much to look through.

Before I leave the garage and search for the phone, I collect all my stuff and spend absolutely ages repositioning the body to a position where I can close the backseat doors. Finally, I am happy with that. Looking at the body, I notice the sparkling gold chain. I swivel it around the neck to find the clasp and unclipped it releasing it from the body. I then put it around my neck and secure it there. I felt that familiar surge of power and accomplishment.

I place the hose through the top inch of the door window and quietly shut both the doors. With my wipes, I clean over the car and place them and the rag in my handbag. Then I turn the car engine back on and leave the garage wearing the jacket and cap still. Slowly, I close the garage door behind me.

Back in the house, I reach up for the phone. Fingers crossed I can get into his cheap Nokia mobile and yes, there is no password attached. Not surprising, for someone like Leers. He does not seem like he'd bother with that kind of 'caper'. Next step is to work out what he has in terms of material possessions that he would divvy out to friends and family. Walking through the rooms again, I study everything in more detail and decide on a few categories. Firstly, the house, then the car, his water sports affects and fishing gear. Searching the phone, it is not easy working out who is who in there, but he does not actually have many contacts. He must have been quite the loner I conclude. It will not matter too much who the messages are sent to as long the cops find that suicide messages are actually sent from his phone. That is the crucial bit. They probably don't bother to cross reference these details with family and friends anyway. That is my guess. Too lazy when it is obvious it is just another suicide. We did not discuss his family and friends, so I wrote the message to state that the house and car are to be split with 'my immediate family' and 'you know who you are' receives the other gear and anything else you all want. I say the usual suicide stuff of 'sorry, please forgive me, I have been having a tough time lately but haven't told anyone so don't blame yourselves' and all that. This message I leave open on the phone but do not put in anyone's contact names because of two reasons. Firstly, I cannot work out the right people and secondly, the moment I send the message to any of them, at least one might take it on themselves to come on over. Not what I want. I settle the phone on the kitchen table. This is smart I think to myself. Suicide note as a text message. Reduces my risk while bolstering the appearance of suicide.

I start wiping down the surfaces in the house with a slightly damp kitchen sponge and I then pour myself a quick straight bourbon into my glass and stand there sipping on it. I wash up the glass, dry it and put it away. I do not want two but only a lone single glass to be found. I finish the wipe down, switch off the lights, lock up the house, check outside for activity and slowly close the door behind me. As I walk to the nearest patch of dark shadow out the front of the house, I listen intently for voices, dogs barking, traffic sounds. Stopping there I smell the air for cigarette smoke, soap, and shampoo. Soap and shampoo odours are indicative of someone in close proximity having very recently had a shower and are therefore probably still awake. Identifying cigarettes in the air is worse as usually smokers are outside and more likely to see someone else who is outside. A scan for the big blue flickering lights of flat screen televisions I found is also useful to see who is around and doing what.

I have inadvertently worked out these techniques to detect who is around, how close, and what people are doing, when out during my late-night wandering through the streets. Quite often, my sleep patterns have been out of whack thanks to the graveyard shifts that I do at the factory. So, at these times instead of lying there for hours in bed becoming increasingly frustrated that I can't just nod off like everyone else on the planet, I get up and take some dark clothes out of the bedroom and into the small lounge room to change into. Stu never seems to know that I am not in bed. At least he has not mentioned it. I will walk around streets at any hour. To combat any fear of attack from losers of which there are unfortunately many around the suburb I live, I always have one of my knives with me and handy too. It might sound strange that I would fear people ready to do harm, people who must be like me, but I am not like them. For me to be involved in any kind of serious physical confrontation that is not on my terms but on someone else's terms, takes the gain out of it for me. So, when I do come across loser like people at night, I avoid them and stay right out of their way. I try and not walk on Friday and Saturday nights when there are way more idiots about. Hot nights I have noticed tend to bring more people out too, like those flying-ant termite things that all fly around in a giant swarm a few hot nights a year, migrating or whatever they are up to.

Shadows are especially useful to become invisible in at night. Even people driving cars with their lights on do not often notice you at night if you stand still and relaxed, enclosed in a shadow, or on the other side of a telegraph pole. You can tell by where their heads face. Shadows are also useful during the day. When I feel the need to turn and look at someone behind me, but I do not want them seeing me do this, I will wait until I am in a shadow before I do it. It is harder to see from a distance someone in shadow than full sun or even half sun. In addition to the patch of dark on the ground, I will also position myself butted up to the object casting the shadow. This way my shape merges with and looks like part of the bush or tree. If a car drives past at any time of the day, it is also easy to time your movement along with it like a goanna hiding in a tree that climbs around and around as you walk around the tree trying to see it. The less people see me and notice my presence the better. I prefer to be as invisible as possible. That way I have the advantage in any situation that might arise. If I see people before they see me, I can evaluate what is happening with them before they can of me. Also, sometimes at night, during my walks I might spontaneously decide to have a look see into someone's house and there is less risk to me if no one remembers me walking along the street just before. Where you place your feet and tread the ground is another important aspect of getting around inconspicuously. Either heel toe or toe to heel placement of feet is important to lower the sound levels of each step. It is easier to slowly place the weight of your body onto half of your foot at a time than the flat sole all at once I have found. Watching where you place your feet is just as important. It is no good carefully walking along only to snap a dry twig loudly underfoot. Leaves are best not trodden on either especially dry ones.

Other reasons for walking with this silent technique is to

DELETING VINCENT

counter any dog barking commotions. Slapping sounds of feet on pavement can alert dogs and often the first one that goes off its head barking, sounds the communal alarm for neighbouring dogs further on down the street. If they do not bark in immediate response to the first one, they are more vigilant and at the ready to do their thing as you walk past. Really annoying. I have discovered there are certain bird species that alert the dogs to my presence in an area too. Masked lapwings are the worst culprits. Especially if they are guarding chicks. If I disturb those birds too much and they start squawking, dogs will often join in too. Birds can be useful the other way around though. They can alert me that someone is moving towards me. If they take off from somewhere in fright because something has invaded their safety zone or territory, they usually fly in the direction away from the stimulus. So, if they fly towards me, I can expect someone or their dog to be coming towards me too.

Getting back to walking quietly. Another advantage is the slight feeling or smugness I get from observing all these people doing their thing oblivious that I can see in their houses or am watching their antics ahead up the street or whatever. Once I started doing this, it just became a habit. So much so that there is one pair of sneakers I hate wearing because no matter how I place my feet, I cannot seem to stop the loud contact smacking sound it makes from my left shoe.

135

CHAPTER 23 AFTER LEERS

NO SIGNIFICANT ODOURS IN THE AIR NOR SOUNDS
so, I head out across the open grass to the roadway. With no
footpath, I walk amongst the trees and bushes growing on the
verge. This keeps me in shadow for at least some of the time.
To cross the main road, I wait till there is absolutely no vehicles
and move fast across, lining up my exit off the road on the other
side with a big bush. If I need to, I can sidle around the bush if
something comes up the street. Nothing comes. At one point
though, I am walking along a side street, and a car does drive
along towards me and there is no bush or any cover. There is
also no way the driver would not have seen me. So as a cover, I
purposefully stride into the nearest driveway and walk right up
to the front door just as the car passes by. Luckily, that house
was blackened with no lights on. The car gone; I continue my
walk back to where I had parked my car. It takes some time, but
it is time to reflect on the enormity of what I've just done. A mix
of emotions. I am feeling that familiar sense of power that I
crave. Power over another. Just to annoy though, my other part
of me is in turmoil and shock all over again. I remember wishing

I could just enjoy the moment without the downer from my self-righteous self, spoiling it. Glinda piss off!

Ơ

As the distance between me and the corpse expanded, I felt safer from the authorities. Every time my moral conscious crept into my head, I blocked it out so I could hold onto and savour the aftermath of my effort. There was extensive planning and preparation and successful execution of the whole entire action that I deserved to celebrate I told myself. The more I thought along these lines the more I brainwashed myself and sold out on my soul. I can see this now but could I back then? No way. It might be because what I felt doing these actions is an intensely elevated level of emotion. A myriad of emotions. Because of the focus I had, combined with these full-on sensations, I do not think I could thing straight. I could not cut through to the reality of it all. I could not or would not listen to what I'd like to think is my true self. The other one. Not the nasty fucked up one, but the empathetic and kind one. This whole idea to take revenge of Vincent started because I was protective and loyal of Debbie. Somehow, somewhere my grip on rationality crumbled away into ashes. I feel completely ashamed explaining all this, especially the nitty gritty details but now I must punish myself. If I do not go all out now with my confessions, of spilling my guts then there is no chance of redemption for me.

Ơ

Thing is, it is too much to explain everything. I just can't. What I can say is to prolong the high, I managed to supress deep inside me the good part that should have won the battle of the brain but lost. At least back then. Brutal Evillene had Glinda by the throat.

As I walked to the car that night, I relived what I did to

Leers in as much detail as I could. This excited me so I kept thinking over it. By the time I reached the car and climbed in, I had worked myself up into a hyped-up state. I didn't want to go home like this and wanting to prolong this mood, I started the car not sure where to go. I had to get out of the street I am in, but I wasn't ready to leave the area just yet. Imagine a spider's web. Even though I wanted to visit the middle of the web and drive by Leer's house, that was out of the question. Logic said I should drive well away from the region and go back home beyond the outer edge of the web. I felt tensions from the middle of the web drawing me there, compelling me there and I felt tensions from the outer threads, drawing me away to safety. Thinking of the two actions in houses, the downside I experienced from choosing those locations is the lack of place to revisit. Revisit the venue to revisit the experience. The car park in the secluded bush worked perfectly for that. I do not remember being aware of this at the time but how I solved this problem was by finding a surrogate site to reminisce at. It had to be connected in some way to the site of the action and it had to be private. Somewhere I would not be noticed easily. Somewhere specifically associated with that particular action and not to be mixed with any of the others. To gain the maximum psychological payoff from these things that I did, I needed to remember as much detail of the whole experience as possible. The last thing I wanted was any mixing of memories between them. Memory mixing sort of diminishes the power and dilutes the excitement. For the high to last as long as possible, I would block out thoughts of previous ones. This allowed me to focus on the details. Annoying memory lapses niggled at me, but I could not do anything about that. I did find though, that the high just did not last as long with each action. I would do everything to grasp hold of the all the aspects, but they would fade and fade faster each time. It then got to the point where it was not so much as a fade from recall but a shift to boredom of some details that used to be the highlights.

I drove around for a while and ended up over at the ocean along a road near a golf course. I pulled up on the side of the road and stopped the car to think and felt Leer's gold chain around my neck. It felt burning hot in my fingers although it could not have been in reality. The excitement and the rush from succeeding in my plan started to flood through me again. I pulled the Barina back onto the road and started looking for a secluded place to park the car. Eventually I found a dead-end road bordered by bush on all three sides for the last hundred metres of the road. No houses with prying eyes. I parked the car facing the exit out, so I can see anyone coming towards me. Fiddling with the chain again, I sat watching the street for a few minutes. Well after midnight now and only a few far away squares of yellow light showing. No streetlights here either.

6

Much time passed but, trying to remember now, I have a memory blank. What I do remember is, the touch of my fingers around the gold chain on my neck and then some kind of overwhelm emotion swept through me. The reality of what I had done hit me as it has done before. Trying to block those bad feelings became too hard. I remember wishing I could stop this whole thing and thinking I should go hand myself in to police and then I would be forced not to continue with it all. That would stop it. Or I should find a psychologist and they might be able to help me. I could say I am thinking of these things but not actually admit to having done them. They could tell me how to retrain my brain, so I will not want to do it. Will not have to do it. Or maybe I should just top myself.

As I later drove out of the street, part of me is thinking how I can now go back to that same dead-end road any time, even during the day to relive the night but another part is saying that I can't go back. I can't do any more of this hatred stuff and I really have to cold turkey or find some way to stop. I am morally way worse than any alcoholic that runs people over and kills them. Alcoholics have problems stopping so how the hell am I going to? Perhaps I could go to some AA classes to get some

139

tips. No, there is no way I am going to subject myself to sitting next to a whole bunch of losers and them think I'm the same as them.

By now I am really feeling pretty crap. It is so hard trying to focus my mind with this stark conflict of emotions. Tears start to wet my cheeks as I drive and my eyes blur. I am not one that cries much so this just adds another layer to my confusion. This is not the me from just hours earlier. Back then I was so in control of everything and another person but now, all you see is a loser mess of a thing. After every one of these actions on someone I do now, the conflicting emotions seem more intense, more confusing, and more stressful. The choice is either to rid myself of the rollercoaster, see sawing of thoughts by simply not thinking or doing any of it from now on, or by unfortunately, working on the next one. I know there will be a build-up. There always is. For a while now I know I will want to relive the night like the other ones. I know it will wear off. The excitement will fade, and I will want more exhilaration. Another rush. The planning and preparation are fleetingly satisfying and gives a sense of accomplishment. But as I know too, each one does not solve my problem. They never rid me of Debbie's round smiling face or the vision of Vincent sneering down at me. They never squash the anguish completely. Only temporarily. That temporary is not long enough. It does not sustain me for long enough. It is never the last one as I tell myself it should be. Just like surfing when I know I should go in to shore because my toes are numb and I am shivering but I say to myself, just one more wave. You can catch just one more and then you may go in. I catch that last one, but I paddle back out for the next last one. So, it goes on and on and I am really not strong willed at all.

The other component of the deviant actions of mine is that I cannot understand how or why I began doing it. The denial enabled me I suppose but that does not explain how I could transfer from not thinking about it in years. If I am honest, I did fleetingly wonder as a teenager what it would be like to kill someone. Then, no big thoughts on the topic until Vincent, when I felt so much anger towards him that I wanted to really hurt him. Then, nothing major until I saw that 'suicided' woman in her house.

Thing with that is, how did I then go from thinking about doing it, to then planning someone else's demise and then to fully go through the act and do it for real? Anger has a large part to play I suspect because that is the dominant emotion I have felt for so long. Anger and a blankness. Emotions besides anger seem to be absent and there is this continual hope in me to just feel. Driving the car fast, sliding around corners, nearly crashing the car, does not even result in any adrenaline injection. Now and then a particularly large wave can make me feel alive but that is about it. Confused, overwhelmed emotions are not at all what I want.

The jobs I have had are not helpful either. They do nothing in the way to help me except pay my bills. In fact, the factory job just rubs my nose in it reminding me how far I have fallen in terms of employment. The bitches there help with fuelling my anger at the world. Or at my world rather. I know I have made this crap life for myself. Now I must work out how to reinvent another life that does not involve taking people out.

CHAPTER 24 RESET ATTEMPT

AFTER LEERS, THERE IS A DEFINITE SHIFT INSIDE me. I know that so many of those clichés they say about serial killers do not apply to all those people. The one I am going to work on hard is that killers can never stop. For the countless numbers of murderers out there whose identities remain off grid, not all, I bet, continue on and on killing people. I know it is not an enjoyable way of living. There is too much angst wrapped up in it. For me it was a matter of be careful what you wish for. I wished for feeling. To feel and not get around in life as just a numb zombi, observing everything and everyone, instead of living. Unfortunately, the feeling bit seemed fulfilling at first, but an angst replaced that misguided emotion. The angst is both to quell my inadequate blankness and numbness, so I am torn to do something to pierce through that. Then a conflicting angst is there steering me away from doing such horrific things to people. So yes, I feel now but it is fucking with my head now. It is not the feeling I hoped for. My aim after Leers is to replace the angst feeling with yet another feeling and not go back to feeling nothing at all.

While standing at the conveyor belt a few nights after deleting Leers, I start analysing my shit. Melita is not on shift that night and Rocky is working another line, so I easily slip into a type of zone-out meditation as I shuffle the food as it rides past me on the conveyor belt. Realisations come to me. One way to feel the right feel is to make new challenges that put me out of my comfort zone. Adrenaline is lacking in my makeup but if I go all out more in a physical way, then that might satisfy me. I mean physical, as in sports.

Two days after figuring this out, a big swell arrives on the coast. My new strategy is ready for testing. In the past, my favourite wave size is around three to four foot high. An innate self-preservation clause exists in all of us, and I aim to bust out of mine and see what happens. Glimpsing the waves rolling along Avoca Point as I park the car, I know this swell is larger than I have ever been out in, with close-out sets of twelve feet high. Instead of watching it as I usually do and bailing out altogether, I peel on my wetsuit and scratch some tread into my surfboard with my wax comb. Looking across at a particularly gnarly looking set, I force myself to feel the angst of the bad crap, the hell crap I have done. I think to myself how this has got to be better. No, I do not want the deviant life. As I am walking now to the beach, I see a surfer get pitched by a wave and dragged across the rocks around the sea pool. Seeing this, a sudden resignation creeps into my head. I must square this in my head. If I die doing this than that is okay because I really do not have much to lose. Reckless though. That is a name to what is going on here, however reckless is not really an excellent choice of word to prime the mind, just before a big wave surf. Especially when you weigh as much as me which is less than seventy-five kilos.

Not gung-ho enough to jump off the rocks out the back, I walk into the rip near the shore and swiftly paddle out. A third of the way out I turn and manage to catch a small one. This is good and I'm up on the sweet spot with my feet, A few turns and the wave is swallowed up by the deep turbulent rip. I paddle back out and settle for a placing not right out the back but around halfway along the submerged reef. A set comes through, and they are of reasonable size. I snag a large one. Well, large for me, but small for the day's session. A get speed on this one and do a smooth cut back before getting off and going back out. By now I am feeling pretty good. Then a massive screamer set comes in and breaks right in front of me. I look at the wall of white water in front of me and yes, freak out internally. I have had plenty of hold downs under the water and I never get used to them. I do feel my heart pumping inside me. This is what I wanted. The wave force hits and shunts me down fast towards the bottom. Over the top of me is the rush of churning water, it is dark, and my board pulls away from my hands. The board pops up to the surface and I climb up my leg rope to haul my body up. Surfacing, there is just a moment to suck down air before another monster wave is over me and forcing me down again. This happens twice more, and I eventually pop up nearly at the shore. Tired, I climb back on the board and paddle out across the white swirl of foam. Not enjoyable, that I have to say. I sit and wait again. Another wave, much smaller than that set comes through and the surfer on it falls off, so I catch it. A few more medium waves come through that I catch and then I am in the perfect positioning for a huge one. As I stroke down the yawning lip and see the big face open out below, yes, hooray I finally feel an exceptional hit of adrenaline. I catch this one and it is so fast I can hardly do anything except hang on. After this wave I feel exhilarated. But then this turns to survival. Another massive wave breaks on my head as I paddled out for more. The board is flung up in the air and wacks me under the chin. There is a ringing sensation inside my head. All I can do is go floppy and be washed around under the wave. I cannot seem to get to the surface, and I feel the energy of the second wave of the set wash over above me. I swim up, take a breath of air combined with seawater and another wave rolls over. I did not even have the energy to try and get under it. Luckily, my leg rope holds fast and eventually I can reach the surface again and crawl onto my board just as a fourth wave collects me from behind. I lie far back on the board and just grip hard with my hands. The wave takes me all the way to the dry sand. Dragging myself up the beach almost dropping my board, I must sit down and get some air. Coughing too. I must have swallowed some water down into my lungs. I am *feeling* though. This is not necessarily a fun feeling but compared to the angst feeling, it is better. It is an alive feeling, well half alive, and that ticks the box. I force myself to acknowledge this as something good. I tell myself that I will aim to do this as much as I can. It might work as a displacement activity at first but hopefully it will end up more than that. I want something that makes me feel exhilarated. Something that is not what I have been doing, to really feel.

ᏮᎶ

I am intent on controlling myself and to feel alive the right way, but in doing so, I end up going into a sort of depression. Even Stu notices so it must be real for him to say something. Usually, I can hide what I am thinking but evidently, I cannot over the next year or so. Again, this emotion of feeling depressed is one that I can do without. Every time I attempt to better myself, I end up falling in a deep hole. Get rid of the angst and replace it with either feeling alive and good or at least no angst and neutral. The cold fear of that blank numb feeling like I do not exist, is what gives me half of my angst. Priority is not to slip back into craving that brief time of false exhilaration. So numb angst I will accept again, but not the death control angst. That is way too much for me. Thing is, I drop down into a different realm of apathetic pissed-off feeling. Counting all the negative aspects of my life puts me in a downer mood which settles in and stays with me. Counting the faults on my fingers, one thumb, two, three, four, and five. By the time I reach the pinkie, six, I really have the shits.

A disturbing and scary thought is that reckless one I had just before going out in the big surf. Thinking that I do not have much to lose and that the worst that can happen out there is that I die. Dwelling on this new way of thinking seeped into my lifestyle. I started to slip. Slip in a new way.

CHAPTER 25 DISPLACEMENT ACTIVITY

AT WORK, WHEN MY FOCUS TURNED TO DETAILS of the fuctory such as cooking smells, and loud machinery roar, I would think of how low I had stooped in my employment status. Once, I had an esteemed and respected job as a veterinarian nurse. My role in that job was of responsibility and I helped animals heal which is a worthy pursuit. Now I was an unskilled factory worker. I could not get a better job. I was lower in rank than the bitches I took orders from. To try and counter this powerlessness, I started stealing more food from the place. I tried to share my techniques with Melita, but she would not be tempted.

"Heh Mel, I'm glad we are on Line 7 again with the pocket pies, I won't have to cook dinner", I said.

"What's that? How come?"

"A few of these go home with me. Enough for Stu and me."

"What? You are kidding right?"

"Um nope."

"How girl?"

"You really want to know?"

"Yeah."

"Just before the break I put one in each of the two pockets of the uniform and store them in the locker when I pull out my food. Then just before we finish, I do the same again, so I end up with four pies. Same with the little quiches," I explained.

"That's so naughty!" Melita said.

"What if you are caught? That'll be it for you. No more job or nothing. You had better watch your arse girl if you are gonna be doing that shit," she said.

"Oh, and do you want to know how to smuggle out the big pies?" I said ignoring her.

"Not really but you are going to tell me anyway, aren't you?"

"Glad you asked", I said.

"Well, you know these blue plastic apron thingies we wear?" I asked as Melita nods her head.

"And you know how we are supposed to chuck them in the bin at the door as we go out? At the end of the shift, I take off the apron and when none of the bitches are watching, I wrap a few pies in it and hold onto it as we walk out.

"Ooops I forgot to throw the plastic out," I said grinning.

"That's enough food to do me and Stu for a few nights."

"Oh my god Ashli, that's so bad, I can't believe you do this! How long have you been stealing like that? No don't tell me, I don't want to know."

"Actually, from the start. Didn't take me long to figure out the technique", I said with pride on my lips.

Stupid me, I thought most of the workers there were doing it but after talking to Mel, maybe not. Just another negative thing I do really. Stealing stuff is another way to make me feel above the system. Anything to not feel like a pleb of a person. My denial is too strong at that point in time to completely shatter this particular immoral behaviour. No matter how sharp my mental knife is, I just cannot penetrate the real me. All the same an apathy overtook me. I did not bother trying not to steal. That's harder. Stealing is a habit, and I can't be bothered with the effort to change that. In fact, my thievery increased in the next few months. As I felt more depressed, my thefts became more brazen. Bunnings is an easy one that I kept taking stuff from too. Those staff are so thick in there that's for sure. Never do I get a rush though. Like at work, it is easier to go with the flow in my head regarding taking things, rather than clamp down, do the right thing, and pay up. I always pay for a portion of it, just not the whole lot. It is not like I plan to steal, it's just opportunities show themselves. For example, one time I took my Woolworths heavy green bag in and placed inside it, a filter thing in a box I knew Stu wanted. I carried the bag around on my shoulder and I was going to pay but then I found myself presenting to the cashier with a pot plant in each of my hands and the bag was, well, back over my shoulder. It stayed that way till I put it in the car. "Gee I forgot I was carrying that" if anyone asked. "Ooops."

Instead of waiting for holidays away, to break into houses, I started getting into a few close to home. Nighttime is a time I found difficult. Not only did I work night shifts but on the nights off, I could not sleep. I would walk the neighbourhood for hours in the early hours. Then, I started driving out to affluent suburbs to walk their streets. It started initially, as a change of scenery because I was bored stiff of the same streets within walking distance from my place. One night, I noticed a particularly expensive looking house with a carport and no cars. No lights lit any of the rooms and old junk mail spewed out of the letterbox. All the signs that no one is at home. Using the cover of shadows, I walked around the side of the house. Concrete steps led up onto a deck at the back. The back door was locked. Moving around the other side, I found a small window next to a laundry door. The laundry door was locked too but I managed to force the window up and open. A chair from the deck helped me prop up high enough and level with the opening so I could thread my body through and into the laundry. Once in, I unlocked the door and put the chair back. Then I walked back in the house closing the door behind me. The owner of this house had expensive and stylish taste. A bit Vogue magazine with clean lines and minimalistic furniture, paintings, and sculptures. Not just a weekender, these people resided here quite regularly I would say. Usually a house like this, if left alone for long, has lamps on timers in view of the street. Hungry, I opened the refrigerator to find it well stacked. Nothing super perishable like milk in there but unopened blue vein and camembert cheese. Blue vein is too costly for my budget but not that night. The cupboard had a whole pack of fancy rosemary crackers to put the cheese on. I just started eating when I heard a faint creaking noise at the other end of the house which made me wonder if someone was home after all. There was nothing obvious in the way of pets around the place. That could be awkward, a vicious dog bowling over to me bailing me up against a doorway or something.

Slowly, I walked along the wooden floorboards and down the hallway in the direction of the noise. Another creak. This came from the roof, so I put it down to just the typical house sounds. Wandering in and out of the bedrooms, all the beds were neatly made with stacks of cushions and oversized pillows. Looks nice but how the hell does anyone sleep with all that? A small office squeezed between two of the bedrooms had a heap of documents strewn around on the surface. Curious, I had a look with my small head torch I carry with me. Bills for that residence, stacked novels, and some share notices from Origin Energy. Boring. Finally, I started to get tired, so I headed back to the kitchen and collected the whole round of cheese and the biscuit packet. I found a plastic shopping bag in a draw, put my midnight snack in there and left, closing the window, and locking the laundry door behind me.

Then I drove to The Skillion to eat my snack in the car overlooking the rocky cove. No one here this time of night, which is how I like it. I thought about what I would have done if I had found someone in that house. My aim for entering it was not to go hurt an innocent person but to just have a look around.

Relieve my boredom. If I had found anyone there, I would have just backed out as best I could and left them alone. One aspect of those types of forays is that I love the fact that I can do this, and no one has a clue about it. I suppose it is a bit of voyeurism on someone's life and their personal possessions but if they don't ever know then that's not going to annoy them. The blue vein made me sleepy, so I headed home.

At least by doing these passive house break-ins, I was avoiding the angst of actions on people. What is missing is feeling though. There is no adrenaline going in and out of another person's house, but I am guessing there probably should be. I was hoping for some boost of energy as a consequence. Thoughts of invincibility and all that but no, it is just another activity to do, like everything else and no different. This lack of high, fed into my overall flat mood that became increasingly familiar to me as every day went on. Still, I was not having to deal with the dark angst and guilt of what I had been doing with those men. I struggled but tried desperately to cling to that thought. Just get through each day and night and things will improve for me surely.

Instead of acting outwards with my anger and frustration at my life and people that continually annoyed the absolute crap out of me, I started to turn inwards instead. This meant bottling stuff up and then releasing verbal outbursts to relieve pressure. Plus, drinking started becoming a big part of my lifestyle. Blotting out my life with that. A spiral of negativity and low confidence in myself led me into a different dark cave than before. The only good thing is, these negative activities of stealing, breaking into houses and drinking replaced the really defective stuff, so in fact I was making progress in a way.

CHAPTER 26 REVISTING LEERS

THERE WAS ONE PARTICULARLY CLOSE CALL,
where I nearly slipped up and indulged back into my old
planning thoughts. The whole week at work was going like
absolute crap. I let fly at the old bitches telling them to go fuck
themselves when they told me what to do with their haughty
patronising tone. Careful not to be sacked, I refrained from
losing it with the Line Supervisors, just the next ones down in
the dumb hierarchy ordering. There is only so much I could take
of their arrogance. My feet were sore that week and giving me a
dull ache and then I started getting throbbing headaches. The
headaches soon became a constant continuous pain. Panadols
took the edge off, so I had them on hand wherever I went. The
headache pain did not seem to feel the same as what you get
from hangovers and all I could do was endure it. The surf had
been flat for weeks, so I had had no exercise, and I really started
to feel pent up. Feeling desperate to inject the feeling of
exhilaration into my life again, to counteract how awful I felt, I
allowed myself to slip. I thought back about Leers and rehashed
the excitement of prowling down a potent stranger. I started to
think how alive I would be if I started planning another.

However, as I trod through the new, rationalising grounds in my head, I managed to pull back from those thoughts. As a reward for pulling back and blocking a new scenario, I allowed myself to revisit Leer's night but keep it at that.

ʘ

It was a Monday night, and I didn't have a shift. My relationship with Stu had sunk to the stage where I would just go out now and not bother to tell him where I was headed or why. This suited me but did not suit him from what I could tell. I figured when I would leave at night, he just thought I had a shift because shifts were at all hours and any day or night of the working week. The length of time varied too. They usually lasted from seven to twelve hours, so it was never predictable when I'd be at work and when I'd be at home.

This one Monday night, I was dreading going back into work to face my degenerate career. I had been binge drinking all weekend at home, feeling sorry for myself which is crazy and just plain pathetic. Stu and I seemed to argue at each other, and we never went out anywhere. To go and do something and grab a chink of aliveness, I waited till it was midnight, crept out and took off north in the Barina. With me was my spray and around my neck was Leer's gold chain. This is not what I wanted from myself. Deep down I knew that I would be feeding the blackness inside me, but denial won. I justified it by telling myself, this was my reward for not going to the next step towards another deletion. I could do just this and not slip back into doing more men. One thing I knew, was that I felt stressed out and I had to do something to relieve my anxiety. This was something I know worked. In the past I only had to do a drive-by of a location such as the bush car park to feel better.

Driving to Long Jetty soothed me. Feeling more in control, I immersed myself in the powerful persona I had created that night. I looked forward to driving past Leer's house and felt a calmness. It did not take long and there I was slowly coasting past his place. I could see a heap of rubbish out on the kerb awaiting the council pickup. Nothing else looked different. Continuing, I drove to my dead-end street I'd chosen to reflect that night. All the houses I passed were dark and quiet. I pulled into the end of the street and turned the car to face the street. Just before I switched off the engine, my mind asked if this was really such a good idea, but that little voice got squashed with, "I'm strong enough now. What will happen if I don't let myself do this, with the high level of stress I'm feeling? Something worse for sure." I took time to go through and remember the details from as far back as the club to really get myself in the all-powerful, dominant mood. A voice reminded me that no way are you powerful, you are a useless piece of shit actually. I kept on until I could remember the conversation with Leers now in his lounge room. An aliveness grew inside me. I fiddled with the chain and sprayed the breath freshener into my mouth and onto my wrist. I also smelt the dry mustiness of the garage and re-experienced the dizziness from the exhaust fumes. Then that weird inexplicable transition of a person existing fully alive and strong, to be, the next moment, completely and utterly gone. Gone and not retrievable at all. Ever.

CHAPTER 27 SUICIDAL

THE MONTHS WORE ON INTO EARLY 2020. THE
more I tried not to slip up, the more I seemed to be propelling
myself to do just that. The more I tried to stop thinking of Leers,
Dave, Byron, Stefan, and Vincent, the more I saw Debbie. I gave
in again and drove by the houses and car parks. My gains from
this, began to fail. Forgetting the most everyday things in life,
due to my lack of focus, became one the multitude of frustrating
things that started to happen to me. I would be driving to and
from work and have no memory of the journey. My angst grew
and the surfing solution was not working.

I started to wonder if I was suicidal. Out of nowhere, I
would see an image of myself diving off the top of The Skillion.
Sometimes it was other cliffs. Physically standing near any cliff,
grew to be a problem for me. Like how trains pull you towards
the tracks when you stand at the platform edge, cliffs drew me
dangerously close to their lethal edges. When this type of
pressure was on the way up, occasionally, I would walk
purposely along the very edges of a dangerously high cliff, just
to let it know who is boss. Looking back now, this was riskier
than I realised.

I am fairly sure I was depressed. My motivation to do the

normal things I liked had dissolved into nothing. Anger inside maintained its red fury alongside a floating feeling of helplessness. The angst grew and all I wanted was the pain of it to stop. The cliffs beckoned.

6

It reached the point where I had wound myself up so much, that I had to relieve the pressure behind my skull, by the only way I knew, but this time with an ideological twist.

To save myself, I had to find someone else to take my place. It was as simple and clear cut as that. Almost like someone had a gun to my head and I had a gun they didn't know about, secreted in my pocket and all I had to do was pull it out, notch back the safety with my finger then shoot them in the temple before they shot me. If I did this, I will save my life. To save my own life now, I needed another person to 'put a gun to my head' or really, I just needed Vincent to make me see red and white behind my eyes and then I had my saviour. From feeling trapped, I now had a way out. Once these thoughts chained themselves together, I became obsessed once again. I needed to find my 'lifesaver'. Who would be my hero and save my life? I didn't want to die but if I didn't release the pressure in my head some way, then I myself would have to suicide somehow and soon. I knew that giving into the hungry desire for power over Vincent would be a relief to the unrelenting and building pressure. The cliff has lost.

CHAPTER 28 NATHAN

IN THE PAST FEW WEEKS MELITA, ROCKY AND I
had been on Bites in the freezer every day and my body just
froze. My grey Adidas track suit pants I wore under the nurses'
uniform just didn't keep me warm enough anymore. I don't
know if they turned down the temperature or the thermostat
was broken or what, but it was torture working twelve-hour
shifts in that place. It could have been because the outside air
temperature remained warm being March, so the difference was
more noticeable. Who knows, but I had had enough, and one
Friday I charged into the Anaconda camping shop at Wyoming
to source some thermal underwear.

Browsing through the clothing there were dark, navy
raincoat pants, and long pants with detachable zipped sections
to transform into shorts but no ultra-warm legging type pants.
In the background, a conversation between a customer and the
shop assistant wafted over to my ears.

"Have you got maps?"

"No sorry mate we don't carry maps."

"Not even ones for round here?"

"Nah you'll have to try somewhere else."

Glancing up, I noticed the customer seemed in his late twenties to early thirties and thin. His cheap attire suggested he didn't have a lot of money. Probably a dole bludger too if he's in shopping on a weekday. Loser, I thought. As he walked out, I followed him into the car park. He did not walk towards a car but towards the main road. I called out to him and caught up as if I too were heading to the main road.

"Heh! Excuse me."

He turned around and stopped to look at me.

"I heard you in the shop just then, where are you after maps of?"

"Oh, up in the bush behind Wyong kind of way. Why?"

"I was just going to tell you how you can get maps of most of the State Forests from the Forestry Department. Um, a bit of a coincidence but I've been planning a trip up in the State Forest for a while now but haven't got around to it."

I paused and tried to look awkward and unsure even though I felt sure.

"Are you from round here?" I asked.

"No near Penrith."

"Oh."

"What are you doing on the coast then, if you don't mind me asking?"

"Yeah, that's alright. Me stepdad is moving back there this weekend and I'm here for the weekend helping with the move."

I paused a bit and then said,

"I'd love some company if you want to do a day trip sometime. I know some scenic spots up there."

"Really? I haven't got a car or nothin."

"That's okay, maybe you could catch the train up and I'll pick you up from the station."

He smiled. I pushed my bust out a bit and he did a fleeting look down.

I pretended to think and then said,

"Actually, I have this coming Tuesday off if you want to go then, after that I think it's forecast to be bad weather for ages."

"Is there anywhere you particularly want to go?

"Yeah, maybe where the dirt bike riders camp."

"The Pines?"

"Yeah, I think so. Me cousins have bikes and talk about riding up there all the time. That's where I want the map for".

"Have you got a bike?"

"No but I'm gonna get one for sure."

"A friend at work rides his dirt bike all the time up there, so I'll ask him where the best tracks are, and we'll go have a look eh?" I venture.

He just smiled again.

"My name is Alison or Ali for short, reaching out my hand to him.

"So nice to meet you Ali, mine is Nathan."

Throwing him a big beaming smile I said,

"Give me your number and I'll ring you Monday night to line up when to pick you up from the station here at Wyoming on Tuesday morning. Just you and me right?"

He obediently wrote his number on a receipt, and we waved goodbye. He kept walking to the main road, and I crossed over and pretended I headed for the fruit shop nearby. I did not want him to see my car in case he talked to someone and described the whole encounter in detail.

CHAPTER 29 SICK

THE NIGHT AFTER MEETING NATHAN, I TRIPPED
and fell while crossing the road and sprained my ankle badly.
Sprained it this time for real with it swelling up and turning
purple and green. I usually always am good at looking where to
place my feet, especially when on a road. This just added to all
the dumb things going on. Sinking further in life, I could not
stop thinking about all the loser things about myself. One thing
would go wrong and then I would mentally count another four,
recent things so then I would have a fist full. Apathy took hold
and the fire in me started to go out. Usually when someone said
something that annoyed me, I would fire back both barrels with
some smart-arse retort to blow big holes in their chest. Now, I
would just stare at them. My immune system must have taken a
dive too because I started to get all the colds and flues that
circulated. Usually, I never succumbed to sickness. That winter
of 2010 I sick in bed for weeks. I would just get over one virus
and then succumb to another. I tried drinking at home when I
was sick but that did not work to cheer me up. It just made me
feel extra bad and for some unknown reason the alcohol effects
seemed muted and therefore pointless. After weeks of no money
coming in, I tried to ignore being sick and took a shift at work.

This lasted all of two hours of solid slog, and I had to wait for a replacement to come in so I could get the hell out of there and back to bed.

Stu would tell me off about my newfound slovenly ways around the house and instead of me arguing, I'd just go 'yeah whatever' to the point where he was the one becoming all uptight and angry instead of me.

ó

One outing to the small library at Woy Woy, gave me a surprising lead on how to change myself. In the past, those self-help guru type books annoyed me, and I thought only insecure losers read that crap. Cynical me, assumed the authors of those books were con people just out to make money creating far out spiels of complete rubbish, and that you had to be gullible fool to believe that any of the concepts could really work. Anyway, this one day that I ventured into the tiny building my headache was back, and I was supremely bored and not in my usual frame of mind. I felt out of kilter. That is my excuse to explain why I ended up in the self-help category. I remember standing there trying to pretend I was not there when an attractive Ryan Gosling looking guy squeezed past me along the same aisle. This happened so fast I did not have time to move along to the next genre to pretend I was perusing biographies and not self-help. If it had been one of the usual demented old people dressed in dowdy tracksuit bottoms and an oversized plain T-shirt, then I couldn't have cared less. What kept me standing there in front of self-help and stopped me from chickening out was a quote that caught my attention from one of the books.

"There is nothing either good or bad, but thinking makes it so."
Written by William Shakespeare.

Maybe I was not so different to those insecure losers vulnerable to weird suggestion, but I reckon the similarity with other readers of self-help is that I know I needed to change, and I had now begun my quest on how to do it. It is not like I could chew the fat on my hellish life with Stu or Melita or Rocky and say "yeah, I happen to have um taken a few lives and now I want to stop, have you any ideas for me?" Also, I could not book into sessions with a psychologist and spill my guts and ask them how to atone and prevent myself doing more. No doubt they would be legally obligated to report me and that would be that. No rehabilitation, just locked up forever. Confined within a building full of complete fuckups all out to get me. No thanks. The good thing about books is that I am comfortable learning via that medium. That started at school and during my Diploma in Animal Care and then as a veterinarian nurse. So many things I have learnt from reading rather than by experience so why not learn how to get out of my psychological pit of hell. I knew I had no choice but to try. My denial had to be scraped off, sloughed away to leave the truth of what I really am. Monster or not. It is time I fully and entirely face this. No more denial.

In the stuffy library that day I selected four of these books and glancing around I had saw Ryan exit the building. Relieved I sidled across to the counter to borrow them and studied the middle-aged, neat looking lady checking through my books for any signs of response to my choices. It is like I thought I'd be found out to be weak. Completely illogical but still that is the level of self-consciousness I had around this fledgling new me. This stayed with me out the main door and into the main street even though the books were all stealthily secreted in my favourite big brown handbag. Instead of my bag carrying the tools of carnage, now they carried the tools of born-again good, or so I hoped.

○

The repeated flu sicknesses timed well actually, because they forced me to stay put and read the books and go through the interactive parts. If I had been well enough to get out and active as usual, and instead of knuckling down with my new resolve, I probably would have run away by leaving the apartment to avoid facing up the dark parts of me. I am not one to believe in fate and things happen for a reason shite, but I did recognise this positive opportunity, and I took it.

I started chugging through one of the books written by life coach, Dr Phil. This is the book with that Shakespeare quote, and it contains a chapter entitled,

"There is no reality only perception."

This concept is what Dr Phil terms as one of "Life Laws" and determines to what level you are happy, peaceful, or satisfied. It involves acknowledging your history without allowing control by it. He goes on to explain how perceptions are how you assign meaning to the sensations you get from the world and that is the subjective part we can change and control. The gist of it, is for me, to work out exactly what has distorted my outlook and then acknowledge it. I must work out where I have gone wrong with my assumptions and fixed beliefs and then take on fresh perceptions that are influenced by fact not history. For me, this is quite a meaty task.

To approach it, I started a little way down the chronological track and then reverse engineered my mindset and actions to decipher my dysfunction. I do at this point accept that to do what I have done I must be dysfunctional. What is annoyingly tempting is that if I interpret Shakespeare's quote literally,

"There is nothing either good or bad, but thinking makes it so."

Then, I could just say, "well my perception of my actions is not bad because it is all in the mind to think anything is bad. It is all in everyone else's mind that those actions are bad. It is all a societal flaw to think things are bad." To be honest, that is what attracted me to reading further from that book in the library. I thought in one sense, this could be a way to feed my denial. I could find external argument to shore up my internal talk and that would take away the shame. Without the shame then I would no longer be stressed. But the more I read from this book the more I realised the truth of me and how I am responsible. The part of me that is the good part, luckily visualised an alternative way of eliminating my stressed state.

6

My background is not one of being in and out of jail, drugs, juvee and all that. I am not someone who gets into fisticuffs around the place or road rage. As a kid I did not torment everyone. I just kept to myself. I would observe people and what went on around me and over time, I formed quite a cynical view of humans. This view is contained within me usually, and people would have no idea what I really thought of them because I would throw them a lovely line, counter to my real thoughts of what fuckups I thought they are. This always made me feel superior.

Something turned me from passive and contained to doing harmful stuff. To relieve myself of stress forever, I had to go hard and examine who and how this went down for me. The one reference point I had to start with is Vincent. His face is in my face at the peak moments of the worst things I have done. Therefore, he is significant in the way I have formed my perceptions. It may all sound easy, but I can tell you it is not. This is hard yards for me. Another disadvantage is I cannot run my thoughts past anyone to get a gauge on it from another person's perspective. There is that word again, perspective. Then I would become despondent, thinking well, how do I know if what I figure out, is really the truth or just another convoluted untrustworthy perception that I have conjured up to deny the real reality. Is it worth the work? Stress verses no stress equals yes; the work is worth it. Circles and loops but progress I did make. That next Tuesday I did not meet Nathan.

CHAPTER 30 STU

MEANWHILE, DURING THIS PERIOD OF SELF-PSYCH examination, my health improved, and I managed to finally start shifts again. This part of my life was both good and bad of course. I hated the humiliation of working in a mundane menial tasked factory but at least I had my friends there. I had missed Melita and Rocky and some of the others. They as always, ribbed me on first shift back and told me I looked like complete crap which was true. Of course, the money helped. I was grateful for my job more than I would realise, as unbeknown to me, the shit would soon hit the fan in my personal relationship at home.

One night Melita noticed my usual chatty self was not that evident and she asked why.

"Oh, Mel you know me, I'm fine", I said.

"But you don't seem right since you've been off sick."

"Yeah, I guess I've been working through a few things," I said.

Usually, I am wary of slipping up with an explanation like that because it just serves as an invitation for more intrusive questions which I do not need or relish like some. To maintain their bonds, women need to share their experiences and that is fine but of course I cannot share even the gist of my experiences let alone any detail. We women like detail. So, I diverted off track and talked about Stu.

"Just stuff with Stu you know, I said," not lying.

"At least you've got a boyfriend unlike moi."

"Well, you don't have to put up with all the shite that men carry on with."

"Like what Ash?"

"All that criticism and put down about not caring enough for him, he wants a fucking mother I reckon. He says he does everything to fit in with my precious schedule and I do jack for his."

I had not been thinking about anything Stu has said to me for a long time really. Too wrapped up in me I suppose. He is right after all. When I said this stuff, it came as much of a shock to me as to Melita. Now a whole string of conversations came back to my ears. I had heard Stu's words, but I had not taken any of it in. My responses back to him were completely devoid of emotion because I had not computed or synthesized any of it. My feeling of flatness and apathy and my self-absorbed attitude probably exacerbated the frustration Stu had. So, thinking back, he had said harsh words.

"You only think of your bloody self these days. You are a user and lazy and thoughtless," he had yelled at me about a week back.

"The only contact you ever want from me is in bed. And then you never look at me, so who is it then? Who have you got on the side? What's his bloody name? Is it someone from work? Is it that Rocker bloke or whatever his name is? Why don't you tell me? You have to tell me!"

"No one, there is no one," I said.

"I left it at that walking out of the apartment and down to the beach. Thing is I did not ruminate on Stu's outburst; I clean forgot about it. It did not interest me. I only left because I could not be bothered doing all the lame patch up talk and bonding relationship crap. He would have thought I went out to assimilate what he had said I suppose but I can't help his assumptions. Probably the other thing that annoyed him was the fact that when I came back, I acted like nothing had happened. This is only because I had forgotten about it and made the huge error of failing to recognise it as a seriously important turning point in our relationship and that I should have paid close attention.

⟳

Disinterest in the right things is one fault of mine and denial is another. One of the self-help concepts I was really trying to get a handle on is denial. The denial I have had about Debbie's death is what I perceived to be the crux of my 'issues.' The guilt I had for not persuading her to leave Vincent. Unfortunately, it was only the catalyst for my descent into hell but around that stage of 2010, I thought it was the core of everything bad I'd done. Working through the rational side of Debbie's death and leaving my personal impressions and interpretations to one side I started to suspect that I had globalised my awry viewpoint of Vincent onto other men. I do not have physical proof that he killed her. That does not mean he did not do it and given his possessive attitude towards Debbie and sneaky aggressive tactics towards me, I am very sure he did put that damn rope around her neck. It was not until much later that I began to realise that I had zeroed in on Vincent from an broad spread of misogynist men in my past. He became a target in my mind. He represented all those chauvinistic men who have made me feel small and disrespected and worthless during my entire life.

Vincent being the target I could not fire upon, because he lives overseas, and this meant other men had to fill in for him. My denial meant I overlooked the reality of Debbie's death and made up my own reality. I deluded myself with the idea that all the wretched men in my life were directly to blame for her leaving and thus deserting me by dying. I felt I should have saved her from her killer. The reality is that he took her life, he took from me the one person I trusted in the world, she did not desert me, and I was never going to be able to help her. I understand that now.

◊

Gradually, I recognised something had changed. Vincent's face began gradually fading from my mind. So was Debbie's. It is like that black lump deep inside me that needed to come out has been regurgitated enough now and is mostly all out and purged. Did this mean I am finally in the clear and will not be compelled to do anymore deletions? I hoped so. The aliveness turned to remorse and shame. With that, the angst came back. Did this all really explain why did I do this to Leers and all the others? I wish I knew.

Also, the worry started creeping in of what really am I? How do I get a handle on myself as a…killer?

CHAPTER 31 STU SHOCK

MONTHS LATER WHEN THE WEATHER STARTED warming up again after an uncomfortably chilly winter, I copped a big shock. It was after a day shift at the fuctory. A twelve hour one. Just a normal day like all the others until I walked in the door to the apartment. For a second, I was sure I had unlocked the front door to the wrong place. But no, I saw the photo hanging on the far wall of Stu and I sitting at a table at his brother's wedding from two years before. I am in the right address. Everything, well nearly everything was gone. Have we been robbed? Walking further in, I saw a piece of paper on the kitchen bench. Feeling my stomach drop I reached for it. It was from Stu.

Dear Ashli,
By the time you read this, I will be a long way away. I don't think we are
a match and I think our relationship was one sided and I just didn't know
it for a long time. I loved you but I don't think you loved me the same way.
Our lease is up, and it is time to move on. Look after yourself. I know you
will.
Love Stu xxx

Shocked, I just stood there staring down at his words. I must have reread the letter ten times before I could move. First thing I did, was try and ring his mobile but the voice on the other end said the phone has been disconnected. I tried to find his brother's mobile number in my contacts, but it was gone. Stu must have deleted it from my phone. He also had removed all his friends, our mutual friends plus his work number that I had stored. I knew the name of the company of where he worked so I looked that up and rang the number. The administration lady politely told me Stuart had not been working for them for about nine months and no she did not know who he worked for now or where he lives.

Wow, how could I not know this stuff? I wandered around and saw he had cleaned me out and taken most of the furniture and the refrigerator. That made me mad. Why wouldn't he tell me he was taking the bloody fridge. It was going to be a hassle for me to get another one and what do I bloody well eat in the meantime? There was no need for that low down kind of act. I was better off without him anyway. I checked the cupboards, and he had taken most of the appliances. I supposed he had bought them not me. He had left some food at least. I checked the bedroom. The crummy Fantastic Furniture bed with saggy mattress ensemble was still there. Yay.

I rummaged on the floor of the built-in wardrobe and under my mess of clothes for my deletion box. Relieved, all the items were left untouched, including a full bottle of Cougar Bourbon that I did not open during that last deletion. As I lifted the bottle off the ground, I wished I could cry. If I could just cry, then I would have some kind of release, but no, that is definitely not something that comes naturally to me. Looking around at the carpet, it was filthy. Stu of course did not bother to vacuum up all the crap left under everything he took from the apartment, and he bloody took the vacuum cleaner too. I had no way to clean up until I bought a bloody vacuum cleaner. Because I had not worked for so many weeks, I was low on cash. Now I would have to pay the entire rent myself too. Maybe I could ride the nicked red bike to work. No, the distance is too far. This whole situation was not making me feel too good. It was too hard to figure it all out. Without even bothering to shower and change from my doughy encrusted tracksuit I had worn to work, I plonked myself down in the middle of the lounge room with the Bourbon and started to drink straight from the neck of the bottle. Stu had even taken the TV! The Bastard.

CHAPTER 32 LIFESAVER MAN

THE NEXT FEW DAYS I FELT LIKE COMPLETE
shite. I had to go to work with a massive pumping hangover and
not decline any shifts because I could not afford to lose the
rental. Lucky for me, Melita was working but on different lines
so I took my breaks deliberately at a different time ensuring I
would not be forced to talk. I was too pissed-off to talk. And
humiliated and yes hurt.

6

Ever since Dave, during the many days of suffering hangovers,
I would always feel extra edgy and paranoid about being caught.
Did I just happen to miss seeing the news that states there is a
current investigation running into the homicide death of Dave
or Stefan or Byron or Shane AKA Leers? Are the police now
hunting for the postie killer? Do I have undercover cars
following me? Are conversations with strangers really innocent?
Or are these people actually undercover officers attempting to
befriend me to trip me up at a later date? Maybe they are now

looking for the sleazy-man serial killer. Often this pressure meant more drinking, stimulating more paranoia, round and round. My existence in continuous loop mode.

As soon as I could manage it, I hauled myself down to the real estate and renewed the lease. Because we had always paid on time and kept the place clean, they did not question that Stu did not sign it too. I did not let on he had gone because I needed them to think I would not have any problems paying. Next thing I needed was the refrigerator and television. I could do without furniture for a while until I had saved enough. No way could I afford to buy take away food, so I had been living off pasta and those cheddar cheese jars and pesto jars. Dehydrated milk powder and stale bread and vegemite became my staples. The sooner I found a fridge the better. My chronic headache came back with force.

Towards the end of the week, I had a day free to go purchase stuff. I drove over to the local commercial precinct at Erina and chose a small bar refrigerator from an appliance shop. I could not wrangle the discount with cash, so I signed for a payment plan and organised delivery. Even though the size was small, the refrigerator would not fit into my little Barina hatchback. The thing that made me mad was the man refused to deliver till next bloody week! Fuming, I threw the car out of that narrow car park and up to the main shopping complex. Flustered I turned left into the first entrance, not realising it went to the underground car park near the back of the ice-skating rink. I vaguely noticed a sign warning there were no surveillance cameras and no insurance for people who park there. I parked in a dark corner and did not get out of the car. I was seething. Life was coming down on me. I tried to pull myself back in line. I failed. I do not know how long I sat there for, and I hardly remember what I did next. It happened in a kind of blur. Everything felt red and angry. The red turned to a burning white. It felt like my head was exploding. I remember a youngish man, kind of strutting along towards stairs nearby. There was no one else but me and him in the car park. Before I knew it, I had unthreaded my belt from my jeans and thrown it on the back seat of the car. Without looking at him as he got closer, I got out of the car and opened the passenger seat door and pretended to try and move the seat. I made a huge deal of trying to move it but not being able to. I opened the door behind as well. After the bloke had passed by me, I yelled out to him.

"Excuse me?" He turned around immediately.

"Would you mind giving me a quick hand? I can't get my seat to go forward and I'm going to be putting a big pot in here behind it", I said with a semi-desperate anguished look.

"Yeah sure", he said walking over to me.

"Thanks so much, you're a lifesaver'.

Softly he said, "Let's see now" as he lowered himself down into the front seat, positioning his body to shift the seat with his weight. He was about to reach forward for the seat adjustment handle under the chair when I sat down behind him, grabbed the belt, looped it into a slip knot and reached over the chair and over his head with the belt and tightened fast. This guy was strong, but I managed to pull back with both my feet on the back of the chair. His hands were around the belt, but he could not fit his fingers between it and his throat. Gurgling guttural noises came out of his mouth but the sounds seem to come from deep down inside him. This I had not noticed in any of the others. I had no time to think about anyone coming close enough to see. I don't think I could focus away from what was happening even if I tried right at that moment. Just before he went, he moved back into the seat and then shifted forwards so hard and with such force that I thought he would break my chair. Last ditch effort got him nowhere and then he left this world. Quickly, I climbed out of the car and closed both doors and walked round to sit in the driver's seat, shutting my door. I backed off the cinch and looked to the perimeters of the open car park before I reached over his head and took the belt from around his head. For what was probably a whole minute, I could not take my eyes away from looking at his dead face. I remember then prodding his cheek to feel the flesh. I always kept a light weight, paring knife in the glove box and I used this to slice a minute nick in the muscle of his right forearm. The whir of a car engine close-by snapped me out of my reverie, if that is what I was in. I do not remember. What the hell do I do now? This I had not planned for. I really don't know even now, what went on then. At that moment however, I did know I had to leave and right away. I tried to reach over to put the seat belt around this person. It had retracted right back so I scanned around and saw a lady walking along about forty metres away. Waiting till she was out of sight, I got out of the car and opened the other front door to rearrange the person body with the seat belt on and positioning it to lean, stabilised into the corner of the door. Reaching into the glove box, I rummaged around till I found my spare scratched sunglasses. I put them on him. Looking okay I thought. Looking a bit like the movie 'Weekend at Bernies' but passable. Gingerly driving away and going super slow with the cornering, I got the hell out of there.

CHAPTER 33 WEEKEND AT BERNIES

THING WAS, I JUST DID THIS THING BEFORE I EVEN thought about doing it. Not good. Not good at all. Now I understand when people say, "he just snapped."

Also, now I had a dead man right with me during the middle of the day. To make my situation worse, I did not know anything about him. Knowing stuff would help me but I'd done it now, so I just had to figure out how to deal with it. Once driving along, the main road and out of the claustrophobic confines of the shopping centre, I put on the radio and tried to relax enough to think. This is not what I want at all. In the past, a lot of time has been invested in how to prevent links to each person and to separate myself from them as effectively and fast as possible afterwards. Now, one of them is fully in my car for all to see! What a stuff up. And in daylight. I'm so used to a cover of inconspicuousness, and this is way out there and the complete opposite. I cannot afford to lose the plot any more than what I already have done. Within all these chaotic thoughts, my mind kept blocking out a recurring sense of shock at myself and

175

confusion. Confusion as to how this had happened. What is wrong with me? Why? These questions impaired my focus, and I really, really, needed to focus.

I try to figure out where to go whilst leaving my actual driving on autopilot. Without thinking, my usual route home from Erina is southbound which is where I find myself driving. I don't remember the details of the drive at all, but I expect I would have noticed if other drivers stared at Bernie sitting right there next to me. Back to my thoughts of what to do. Looking over at Bernie's neck, there are obvious dark red marks where the belt buckle dug into the flesh with the struggle. This means I will have to either make sure he is never found or if he is, it's after some kind of physical deterioration to the level of skin and muscle decay, ensuring the marks are never seen. I am thinking burning, acid or something. Problem there is, doing that in a way that looks like by natural causes is too hard for my frazzled brain to work out. If I drive up into nearby mountains, I will not know where to go, or where my crap little low to the ground car could even go without getting stuck. Also, we had a heap of rain recently making the dirt tracks possibly muddy and slippery. Not a good look to go up there and get bogged with a corpse. My mind whirring from one thing to another, and my headache really laying in the boot, all I could manage was to drive towards home.

One thing in my favour is Stu was no longer around. This gave me a breather. Since he had left me, I had been parking my car in the narrow single garage adjoining the apartment. I had forgotten about this. There are twelve garages all separated by brick walls with visual and mostly sound privacy. They are not odour proof though. As I drive closer, I am thinking I can just park the car in the garage until I work out what the hell to do. As I am just about to pull into the driveway, I see two neighbours standing around gasbagging about nothing and a bunch of teenage long-haired boys walking along opposite, so I gun the motor a bit and coast away. The problem here is, I must get out of the car to raise the garage door. Anyone close by may well see two people in the car and notice that no one walks back out of the garage with me afterwards. It takes me four drives past before I finally have a clear window of time with no one around. I raised that garage door so fast it clanged loudly but there is nothing I could do. As I lowered it after parking, I saw no one around. As a precaution I did not stay in the garage although I wanted to, I just walked out like usual, then calmly checked the mailbox for mail. I had to focus on the appearance of normality.

Once inside, first thing I did was use the loo and then pour myself a calming Bourbon and coke, took one swig and my phone rang. It was work wanting me to come in for a 2 am shift next morning. Without being able to think, I said yes that is fine and ended the call. As I was saying the words, I realised I had to drive there in my car and how the hell could I do that? This kind of tension I did not need. How do people handle this shit? Is this why people are caught? I cannot be one of them. I am not going to be one of them. I will have to work this out.

To think straight, I had to eat. The motions of cooking pasta calmed me down. I delayed thinking until my belly was full. Sitting down on the one, white plastic, outdoor chair that Stu left me, looking at the dirty wall where the refrigerator should be, made my anger resurface. Anger is not useful right now. That is what got me messed up in the first place. Anger at Stu and the mess he put me in. Anger at those idiots refusing to deliver my refrigerator. I poured another stronger drink. Early afternoon it was by this time. I had about twelve solid hours to dump Bernie somewhere. I tell myself I am smart and that there is no reason I can't find somewhere, some way. No more drink for me. A clear brain and no impaired driving on the road later, is what I must have. I could not risk erratic driving to attract unwanted attention from the cops.

CHAPTER 34 PANNO BOY

THINKING ABOUT WHAT WENT WRONG HERE AND how I ended up 'snapping,' I vaguely remember a similar incident as a child. Maybe if I could recall that and what made me 'snap' then I had a chance of preventing myself from falling into this dire situation again. If only those idiots had done what I asked and done the delivery, then this would not have had to happen. If only Stu had not left me. If only he had left me all the stuff. If only. If only. I am so accustomed to blaming other people. It goes on and on. I do know that I tend to count crap events on my fingers and when I reach my little pinkie finger, I fire my anger right back at the world, usually in some nasty, contemptuous way.

At school, there was this occasion where things were not working for me, and the pressure built up and up. A certain group of older kids had been hassling me for months. Because I bit back at them verbally, they kept on at me. One boy, this black-haired kid of Italian descent everyone called 'Panno' by shortening his last name of Panetta, took me on as his personal entertainment. Not satisfied with just a battery of nasty sexist words, he eventually started trying to touch me in inappropriate places. School became a nightmare. Every time I had to set out across the school grounds to my next classroom, I had to be on the lookout for this complete shithead. He would appear from behind walls or be right behind me from out of nowhere and then if he could, he would turn towards me blocking other people's view of me and go to put his hand up my skirt or squeeze my breast. My breasts back then were larger than most of the other girls my age. As he was a solid sized boy, it was easy for him to pin me up against a wall and position his torso to make me disappear from the other kids and teachers. Telling him off just made him laugh and smirk at me. Once, I stamped hard on his foot, but he just laughed harder while he grabbed some of my stomach flesh and twisted it tight giving me an angry purple bruise that lasted more than a week. I felt humiliated about what this jerk was doing and could not tell anyone. My friends knew I had issues with him but never saw the sexual stuff he did. There was no way I wanted anyone to think I was weak, so I made sure they never found out the full extent of it.

This one day though, I was having constant arguments at home with mum, Panno was relentlessly on my case and had nearly managed to get a hand down my undies that morning when I was walking into the girls' toilets and then my history teacher decided it was time that he had a rant at me. All I had done to warrant this unjust tirade, was inform him that he had made a mistake with my exam marks, and it was unfair that he would not rectify his error just because the rest of the class was being noisy. As his angry voice kept droning on and on at me, my mind switched off to his words and my anger built and built. The injustice of it all fuelled me right up. This overall feeling was that I had no control of what happens to me, day in and day out. I could feel other students' eyes on me. No sympathetic vibe though, it is always everyone fend for themselves when we were up against a teacher. On and on he went. I could feel the red fill my eyes and wash over my whole being. The red turned into a white trembling heat. Then I 'snapped.' I couldn't think anymore, I just stood up and with all my strength, I pushed the wooden desk, fully over in front of me, nearly injuring some kid in front. Then I picked up my chair and threw it hard at the wall next to me. I grabbed my bag, leaving my exam paper on the desk and stormed out yelling that he was a bloody useless teacher. I walked out of the school even though it was before lunch, and I went to the nearby park for a while before going home. That of course got me a lengthy suspension and if I had been at a private school, I would no doubt have been expelled. This was near the end of term and lucky for me, Panno prick moved away during the summer holidays and his friends knew about my furniture outburst, so they mostly left me alone. The worst I copped from them was they would sometimes call me a 'fruit loop' or 'fruitcake,' 'loony tune', that kind of thing. My only regret was I did not figure out how to squash Panno when I had the chance.

So, the 'snapping' with that teacher matched the identical sensation to what I felt in that car park. The terrible and tragic difference though was Bernie was completely random, and innocent and he lost his life for nothing. There was no provocation at all from him. He even was a nice guy helping me so I cannot understand why when I snapped this time, it was not at a specific individual that angered me somehow.

Managing to remember this and draw the similarities together really did not inform me enough to allow me to work out how to prevent me losing the plot again. Again, there was a level of denial that I could not shift. I would reinforce to myself that if all the men were not so arrogant and if they did not try and control my life, then I wouldn't end up doing my crap back at them.

CHAPTER 35 DEALING WITH BERNIE

AFTER EATING, I COULD NOW THINK. DARKNESS
was the best time to remove Bernie from my car somewhere.
That meant I had from around seven to eight o'clock onwards
till say one thirty in the morning when I would have to make my
may to the fuctory. Ideally it would be closer to the one-thirty
am mark as there would be less people around. I could either,
drive a long way and offload earlier in the night, before
midnight, to allow time for me to drive back home by early
morning, or I could find somewhere close and exploit the post-
midnight period with scarce people out. The other aspect is, if
this one is discovered too far from the region, more suspicion
may be drawn to the cause of death. Marks on the neck are
visible so either it cannot be found or at least if it is found, the
body needs a way and time to decompose to hide the exterior
wounds. I will not be able to mask this as a suicide easily. I
cannot wash away the bruising. Oh, hang on, maybe I can. The
ocean can work wonders on dead flesh. Lots of mutton birds
have been washed up on the beaches lately. They fly over from

Siberia, I think it is, on their way to nesting grounds in New Zealand. Any kind of storm wipes a lot of them out and their dead bodies line the beaches, their carcasses in various levels of decay. I imagine what a human might look like after floating about in a salty sea for a while. Even better, a big carcass might just end up sinking deep down, never to be seen again. As I am thinking this through, I remember looking out at the ocean recently. Trawling back in my memory I see that grinning annoying bloke sitting in his car next to me at The Skillion. It is not a long distance from the car, over the rocks to the ocean edge from where I parked that day. There is no big barrier in front of the car either. Just low sandstone boulders to prevent cars driving off the edge and onto the rock platform. The risk here though, is first that someone might see me doing this and secondly, what if it washes back in too soon? My punishment for being a hopeless idiot and gone and done this erratic and again terrible thing, is I'll have to take the risk. The alternative is work up a better plan with more time. Ring in sick and store it in the garage. That is not good either given that there will be a smell eventually. Also, I might not be able to drive the car and have it looking like a person after too much time has gone by. The main deciding factor is the panic and urgency and my need to end this tension. One good cover detail in my favour is that my neighbours are familiar with me leaving at all hours to go to work.

I need some sleep before this next shift even if it is only a few hours. First, before I can relax and do that, I go and check the car. After closing the garage door behind me, I open the passenger door, and bend over the body sitting up in my car. Pressing the palm of my hand into the arm, I notice the tone is firm now, not the flaccid viscosity of the just dead, nearly alive but not anymore. The colour of the face is an unattractive shade of grey. I take the sunglasses off and the eyes have changed too. They are a bit like glass eyes of the blind. Fixed and staring but without focus or detail. The eye parts are just merging together inside the eyeball. I unclip the seatbelt to lean the whole thing forward to search for a wallet and I find a well-worn black nylon one with Velcro fastenings in his back pocket. This is not something I want to look at, but I must, to decide whether to leave it on the body or delay identification by taking it. I decide to put it in the glove box and work that bit out later. The marks round the neck do not look good at all. This reinforces my resolve to follow through with my plan tonight with the ocean location. Propping the body back properly in the car and refastening the seatbelt, I shut the door and leave the garage. Satisfied that there is nothing else now to be done till I drive out, I go and sleep for a few hours. Surprisingly, after setting my alarm my whole body feels drained, and my tiredness takes over.

Waking with a pounding heartbeat as my alarm sounded off and pulled me from a deep sleep, I dressed quickly and decided to take a beanie, torch and my belt I used yesterday plus a plastic bag and my handbag. The wallet would also have to go in the bag too. I remember this distinctly but later I cannot remember what happened to the wallet or the belt. There is a complete void in my memory as to what I did with these things. This scared me then because I did not know if someone had taken them from the car or I'd left them somewhere unsafe and risky or what the hell I'd done. It scares me even now because I can't be sure of every single thing I have done out there. I cannot pin it down either to say experiencing a memory blank when my fierce headaches come on or something like that. It is a blur in my life. A very scary blur. One thing I am quite sure of though, is that because of the deep and shameful, bad feeling I felt about what I had done to this man, there was no compulsion to take anything of his. Vincent was nowhere to be seen.

After fitting the beanie over the head and tucking the excess hair under it, I drive the car out, close the garage and drive away from the apartment, I am again amazed, at this real person sitting in my car next to me. Again, this confronts my denial of what I have done, and I feel horrified at myself. I do not put the sunglasses back on because it is so dark and that would look wrong, but I think the beanie should help to mask any recognition of who this is I'm driving around the place.

Glancing down at the fuel gauge, I notice the car is nearly

out of fuel. This puts me in a spin. Why didn't I realise this before? Repeating in my head, the three favourite words my mother would inevitably use when she was not happy with me, for even the most miniscule misdemeanour "Bloody useless Ashli!" I cannot risk filling the tank with all the cameras at those service stations. Bernie might not appear to look like a Bernie under scrutiny. But do I risk running out of fuel before I reach the rock platform? Opting for hope that I won't run out of fuel, I slow my speed right down to make it last the distance, and head north towards Terrigal. The night is quite dark. A cloudy sky blocks the sliver of a moon. Only a few cars are out, probably because it's early in the working week. A calmness has come over me as I force myself to slow my driving. I find reggae music always helps me relax. I usually have music such as "Third World" or "Bob Marley and the Walers" playing in the car to help me wind down on the drive home after work. I put on Bob and up comes the song; I shot the Sheriff. This makes me question myself about how I will react tonight if I get pulled over by police for some random reason. I always have that small discrete, paring knife in the glove box of my door, in case someone hassles me or conversely, I need to spread vegemite on a sandwich. Would I panic and use my knife? Would I respond like those types of people, who go and hurt a police highway patrol officer, to prevent a car inspection, and then escape with a pursuit? Or would I keep my cool and try and use female charm as deflection away from what is sitting in the chair right next to me? These are the type of scenarios I prefer to have pre planned in my head. Planned, organised well in advance and before the time I might need to follow through with the action I had settled on. It is all a bit too close to the bone right now, so I skip to the next song. I stop thinking about it and pretend I am just driving with nothing else in the car. All is going smoothly, until I drive along too fast around the corner just before Lizottes Restaurant before the Avoca Beach turnoff. The curve in the road sweeps to the right and then banks to the left. Fine if you are going less than sixty kilometres per hour. Faster than that and its tight. As I took the turn, Bernie tips over, half into my lap. The seatbelt is holding half of him upright, but he is looking completely wrong for a passenger. No one in the revision mirror, so I pull off on the next verge. I turn off the engine and kill the lights. Just as I am shoving the whole thing back over, a police car incredibly does drive past. Remaining immobilised, I wait to see if they turn around. After long minutes tick past, there is no sign of them. I resume pushing the whole thing into the corner of the door for support. I really want to tighten the seatbelt, but I cannot reach far enough, and I don't want to risk getting out of the car. Driving off again, I make sure I tone my driving down a notch more, especially the cornering aspect.

Arriving at the Skillion, I drive in and commence the one-way loop around the oval towards the headland and rock platform. All the time, I am looking for any other cars or people but there is no one. I am in luck here. It is well after midnight and as I reach the tiny rocky cove to the left of the rampart, I am grateful there is no extra lighting here. Its cosy dark. Parking exactly in the same slot as before, I peer out into the headlight beams, to gauge the swell size which is big enough for my plan. Then I lower my window so I can hear anyone coming, switch off the lights and turn the ignition key to completely off. Sitting there I think through what I am about to do, choosing which pathway to take the hulking body out across the rock piles and rock platform. The sea can then swallow up my mistake and take it out and away for me. All the while, I am looking in the revision mirror to check there are no interlopers to the area around me. A space that I need to have as all mine, for these next few crucial minutes. Hearing traffic on the main road, I turn to look, but the headlights go past and up the hill rather than into the loop road I am on. Thinking about what they can see from that viewpoint and imagining the process of dragging the body out of the car and along the rocks, I realise if I repark the car, backed in toward the sea, the passenger door can act as a barrier to anyone looking in our direction. Without turning on the lights, I turn on the engine and repark, backing in, lining up the left side as best I can in the dark, with a gap in the sandstone boulders. Switching off the car, I sit and waiting and listening. I tell myself I can sit here forever but I must do this and now.

I take the torch and put it down my bra because I do not have any pockets. Without making any rushed, fast, or jerky movements that might draw people's eye down to me, I get out of the car and quietly close the door. Moving right around the back of the car to the passenger side, I glance down at the swirling frothing menacing waves pounding onto the rocks. Through the darkness, I can make out an obvious trench between the rocks that is like a monster's tongue that can retract and carry its food back out to the ocean stomach. I am thinking I want it to float away rather than sink too soon. After opening the passenger door fully, I reach down and remove the heavy boots and socks from the feet and leave them in the foot well. I start hauling Bernie out of the seat, which is really difficult. I drag him across the ground between the rocks and down towards the ocean. By pulling and locking my arms under the armpits, and walking backwards, I can manage his stiffness and heavy weight, plus importantly, facing the land, I can see if anyone drives along the loop road and sees what I am doing. Down at water level, I am confident that no one can see anything from the main road on the hill. Slow going but I can do it.

During a breather, I pull the torch from my bra to see how far I can safely go out, along the wet rocks but I nearly drop it. I then hold the torch in my mouth, clenched between my teeth. Wave noise is now too loud for me to hear any cars potentially coming. Suddenly, the water sucks back and the trench almost runs dry. I wait for it to refill. As soon as it does, I haul the bent body over into it, forcing it headfirst, right into the water, and pushing with my steel capped boots at the bare soles of the dark looking feet. After accepting its offering, the giant tongue retracts back and takes Bernie with it. Switching off the torch, I go to the side of the rock platform and sit behind a rock shielding the view of me from anyone passing by. I watch the swirling, swashing of the ocean. My eyes adjust to the dark. Once I see that the trajectory of the body continues out in the direction of the open ocean; to be then picked up by the southerly swell, I quickly walk back along the dark rocks to the car. As I walk, I consider leaving his shoes and socks neatly at the rocks edge or even up at the top of the Skillion. This would imply suicide. It would also prompt a sea search which is not a desirable outcome. A search is fine if it is far into the future though. It does seem a waste of opportunity to show the versatility of huicides. Reaching into the foot well, I bend down and while leaning over, I pick up a boot and inspect it with the torch. They are well looked after. Redback brand leather boots with an unusual redback spider imprint in the soles. Picking up the socks and boots and turning off the torch, I quietly close the door and walk to the base of the Skillion ramp. Stopping, there is no one at all close so I quickly walk right to the top. Puffing from exertion, I stand still to recover my breath and just to my right, I notice a large thick bush growing near the main first fence. With one sock, I rub the entire surface of both boots. Under the bush, I neatly place the shoes and socks. One day down the track, they will be discovered, but hopefully not too early to instigate a sea search. Walking fast down the ramp and across to the car, there is still no one around. Numb, cold and relieved, I drive away. Rolling down the steep hills in neutral gear, I managed to make it home without refuelling.

CHAPTER 36 FAYE

WHEN IT COMES TO DEBBIE'S DEATH, I COULD
not relate to that distraught man in 2007 that said,

"She's in there, my girl, she's killed herself." If only I had
believed Debbie took her own life. Then maybe I would not
have gone to hell on earth.

"Maybe her pain just got too much for her." How things
would have been so different if that were the case for Debbie
too. If only people knew what I knew. It was my job to make
people know. My duty. My redemption. Or so I thought, until
Debbie's mum, Faye rang me one cold and rainy morning. This
single conversation altered everything.

We used to be quite close but lost contact after Debbie's
funeral, so I was surprised to hear her voice. Bypassing small
talk, she went straight to the point. She told me how she was de-
cluttering her house and sorting one of her bookshelves where
she had placed Debbie's books after she had passed away. As
she took one of Debbie's novels off the shelf, a photograph
dropped out of it and onto the carpet. The photo showed
Debbie's two cute dachshund cross puppies that she had
rescued from the RSPCA. These two puppies went missing

about two weeks after Debbie took them home. At the time, she said she thought they must have just escaped through the fence and become lost. They never returned home. On the back of the photograph, Debbie had written in blue biro,

"Vincent killed Toby and Sunny. He cut into their throats with a knife in front of me and told me this is what will happen to me if I speak against him ever again. I will be silenced forever. He put them in the garbage bin."

Faye then told me how she typed Vincent's full name into the internet, and up came a list of news articles from Washington DC about his recent arrest. I told her how I had periodically searched up his name every few months for years but only ever found details regarding his Psychiatry practice on Wisconsin Ave, in a place called Tenleytown. She then told me Vincent had "allegedly" murdered his new wife and had made detailed attempts to stage her death as a suicide. I felt like my stomach had dropped out of me. My mind started whirling. I can now see Debbie's face clearly, framed by her unique blonde and frizzy hair. The mixture of fear and the hint of defiance. 'Eggshells' she would say. When she let her guard down with me, occasionally she would describe feeling like she is treading on eggshells when Vincent was in the house with her. This face I can see, is not sad and depressed but tense, fearful and a smidge angry. Absolutely not the vibe of a suicidal Debbie. I just cannot believe how this shifts everything. People will finally now know Vincent really is her killer. It is too coincidental that Vincent has serious relationships with two young women who are decades younger than him and that they both take their own lives. The world will know huicide is very real and happens to actual people. Either Vincent got sloppy or those police in the US are applaudably diligent.

Even though my mind was made up about Vincent physically killing Debbie, there was always a small amount of doubt about whether that was the truth. So, I am very relieved that Faye and I, two people who were mother and friend to Debbie now know that the act of living meant more to Debbie than dying. She never abandoned us. She never did take her life.

She never suicided.

CHAPTER 37 ALL THE MEN

EVEN THOUGH MY HEAD WAS A MESS, THINGS started to gradually crystallise in my brain. I am now sure. All these men are Vincent.

Vincent both emotionally and physically attacked Debbie, but she did not give up. Vincent staged Debbie's death as suicide, therefore I wanted Vincent to die by suicide. As payback. Or for redemption for my failure to protect Debbie. Only I could not make that happen to him, mentally nor physically. I did not have access to him. Plus, he was not the type to top himself. The proxy that must have evolved somehow, deep in my subconscious, was to pretend that he suicided and died. That is as close as I could get. Close enough. That is what will avenge his horrible treatment and total annihilation of my friend. I wanted him to feel the death that she felt. I could not replicate the mental angst but maybe I could replicate the physical side of it. I wanted him to feel the physical side of death. Feeling death would be enough. A man that seemed like him. Is him. Is him but isn't. A man like him feeling death. A man like him feeling death would be enough. Only, it wasn't.

Hearing and processing what Faye said about Vincent is

weird. It is now as if I replicated his atrocity to other victims of his and not to him. Thinking about the ramifications of this makes me feel absolutely nauseated. (Even now, decades later).

Thinking it through further, I realise what it all really means. Me, by copying his actions, means they are not victims of his, all those men are all victims of mine.

Going back a step into the 'what-if' territory. What would have happened if the world had known the truth about what Vincent did to Debbie from the get-go? Would I have gone down this jagged, warped route to hell if I had known that after he had physically killed Debbie, that he would be caught, known, and punished? Emotionally destroying her and driving her towards a breaking point before physically killing her, somehow seems more preventable, more torturous, and more worthy of punishment than a murder minus the mental torture. I always felt extremely guilty that I did not manage to stop him from all the psychological abuse and then her murder. Perhaps that is what twisted around, all black inside me, like the rotting dead intestines of a colicky horse with a twisted bowel.

That guilt that has eaten away at me and is now completely squashed. Squashed and gone but replaced by all my guilt of all the innocent men. I am like Vincent. Only much worse.

To answer that question about my recent journey to hell, feeling these emotions of shock, shame, guilt, and absolute regret, I doubt that I would have done those acts if others had knowledge of the truth. If though, I suspected that he had indirectly murdered Debbie rather than directly killed her, and no one else knew, and he was getting away with it? Realistically, and ashamedly though, I really cannot be sure. The fact that he is now caught means he is likely to suffer. That offers me strong feelings of satisfaction of his impending punishment. That omits my requirement that someone else is punished.

What this understanding of myself meant was that I no longer felt compelled to keep staging suicides. My urge to continue doing what I had been doing and presenting Vincent's huicidal actions, were absolutely blown out of the water. What does remain though, is my hatred for the personality type of

Vincent. I loathe and still despise these types of men. That did not change with my revelation. I reached inside myself and ripped out the notion of *all the Vincents*. Even though Vincent physically killed Debbie, it is now known, so he will now suffer and that is all. That is enough. Vincent is now DELETED.

CHAPTER 38 THE WICKED WITCH

VINCENT **IS** DELETED. A CALM SETTLED INSIDE ME. That Tuesday when I did not go and meet Nathan for our fatal foray into the state forest was the start of my turnaround. I knew instinctively that that decision if I had to make it again now, would not need to serve as a test of my resolve, thanks to my absolute lack of desire to hurt him. There is no hitting that *undo* button. For weeks after Faye told me the news, the words from the "The Wizard of Oz" movie became stuck in my head; "The wicked witch is dead!" Mulling over the phrase, it took me more time than it should have, to realise that that witch isn't Vincent, the Wicked Witch is me!

Tests of witchy resurrection came and went with the usual psychological pressure of arrogant men. They annoyed, they frustrated me, but they did not penetrate and provoke any anger. So much of my anger had diminished. Not all, but most. The red-hot angry portions had gone, vanished without trace. Anger downgraded to annoyance. I would say it is because I now understand how I irrationally linked all the arrogant males from my past to Vincent himself and how insanely stupid that is. It is like all those chauvinistic, misogynous slights thrown at me for the duration of my life meant all those males accumulated together as one and became stored inside Vincent himself.

Setbacks did and still happen today. Such as the time a usual, prime target type, a haughty fifty something man drove through a stop sign and t-boned my little old beloved car crushing the whole front end with his pretentious Jaguar. No apology from him nor even a check to see if he had hurt me. Yes, I became annoyed, but the anger was absent. As I waited for the tow truck, I waited for the anger. It never surfaced. I noticed too how my mind felt clear and in complete control. Another realm where frustration fails to switch over to seething anger is surfing.

Mind you, it is not like it is all easy, there are things I do to avoid risking a relapse. Each time I make effort it strengthens the right feelings. For example, the first sign I notice a male surfer snaking people's waves, I paddle far away to avoid any interaction. Over time, the friction I used to experience from dickheads like that, has smoothed out. There is an acceptance I now have of this behaviour purely because I recognise it to be just that. A behaviour. No longer do I react in a personal way. These types of behaviours are inflicted upon people all the time and really are not a significant thing in the big scheme of life and lives. Lives are more important. Lives are important. Analysing the big picture of life and death and men and women has given me an important perspective that really has changed who I am. Maybe that's what people mean when they say they are "born again" Christians or whatever. My feeling is that all that I did that was horrific and horrible is almost like from a past life. I am not denying at all what I did and how very wrong it was, but it is like I am looking at that girl through the eyes of another girl while standing opposite her. The old Ashli is ashes. Even if Vincent is freed one day, I am confident in my mind that he will permanently remain deleted. No restoring that hard drive, ever. This is what I hold onto daily.

6

Peppermint smell and taste I very nearly gag at today and I cannot handle walking in the bush in or after rain due to that horrible tang of wet eucalyptus. Too many associations which started with Dave, that deeply repel. When these emotions flood and overwhelm me, I squeeze my left bicep where my tattoo is and transport myself to a room with a bed where I can imagine lying down next to Debbie. She is happy and peaceful, and I start to feel at ease again.

Every day I think about and regret descending into hell and doing everything that I did. My mind goes into painful ruminations thinking about Bernie in particular. Both Bernie and Stu treated me with a certain gentleness I repelled myself against. It is like I wore a thick plastic shower cap on my head to block that silky feel of water on the scalp during a warm soothing shower. Perhaps I thought they were foolish to treat a lowlife undeserving girl like me with such unconditional kindness. Why did I not understand who Stu really was? I so wish I had. These types of men I can now see everywhere in the world. In fact, the streets are full of people willing to be kind to each other, expecting naught back. Now my eyes are open, I am learning from them. Instead of the dark I used to only see in people, I now can now see their light. I understand this at last. It is meant I have managed to experience connections with people that are based on the multitude of good in life and in humans. To discover more and be active about this, I decided to work as a volunteer in my favourite clothing charity shop.

It was nearly going to be the Greyhound Rescue Group I would volunteer for, but I realised it's people I really need to form normal new and positive bonds with, not animals. No past stuff to cloudy my future either. I have remained detached from humans most of my life and it is now time for me to reattach. It is time for me to feel, accept and reciprocate the care and love of others. Resigning from the veterinary job was one positive step I have made in my life, and I have now made another most important step.

I visualised those dogs grinning and happy on lounges. I can now see myself sitting on my couch next to people deep in conversation. And I can also see an overweight tan Labrador sharing the couch with me. If I play my cards right, I just might be lucky enough to be happy and content in relationships with people that care about me. Plus have my own dog to love.

ტ

At present I work at the charity shop for one day every fortnight. It may sound odd to most people, but the degree of care total strangers demonstrate to others continues to amaze me. And I do not think they are acting just to ensure they go to heaven or manipulate the other person in some manner. If there is a God, I may not be going to heaven but at last, I am no longer living in complete hell while here on earth.

One relationship that I cherish is one that seems unusually easy and natural to me. It is with a Caucasian pudgy middle-aged bloke I work with at the shop. Mutually platonic, we often share dinner and a beer together in the open courtyard at the Hotel Gosford pub. I admire this man's genuinely caring and tolerant attitude and his depreciating sense of humour. He has illuminated for me everything wrong in my previous deep-seated interpretation of people and life. It is like I can feel again. I can finally feel like I really am here in this world and I do exist. Exist devoid of angst.

Paragliding has become an obsession for me. A better way to feel alive. Every spare dollar I earn, I spend to fly high up in the sky. Presently, I am saving to buy myself a new paragliding sail to float around above the sapphire ocean and jumbled cliffs at Crackneck Headland. The grassy take-off slope is close to where I now live, and the surrounds are spectacularly steep with rugged scenery. The camaraderie among the fellow paragliders is high and I appreciate how these men look out for me with technical gear tips, weather knowledge and plain and simple fondness. I became hooked on flying after my first tandem flight a few years ago. After a series of lessons, I purchased the instructor's old gliding kit that was slightly too large for his petite wife.

6

I may have changed hugely with a positive trajectory, but I am also brutely realistic. In facing up to me, I have created a caveat for myself, designed like flicking on a pistol's safety catch to protect other people. This safety catch has functioned as the number one priority in my life since Faye's phone call all those years ago. It is actively maintaining the knowledge that when I die, I will not have deleted anyone else. This is I will admit, still somewhat a work in progress even today as I write this. Underpinning the safety catch, I locked in an – "if this, then this" - automation into my whole being. If things for me do change again for the worse and pressure and anger begins to build again and I feel flashing bursts of dangerous fury, then I will not find and delete another lifesaver or anyone else, I will hit my own delete button.

6

About to write the two last words of my confessions, I know I am not finally released nor have I no dark pain. What I do know is that I am hundred percent, undeserving of total freedom from this pain, until my own death.

THE END

ACKNOWLEDGEMENTS

A huge thanks to Karin Cather who conducted a thorough plot evaluation. Karin's evaluation was invaluably through the eyes of both a Prosecutor and an Editor. Her feedback came accompanied by useful true case examples. Not just technical recommendations, Karin also imbued me with confidence in my writing, which is something that can be fleeting while producing a novel.